FIRST LIGHT

Animal Voices in Concert

Ardeth De Vries

PublishingWorks
Exeter • New Hampshire

Book layout, front & back cover designs:
    Grant Dunmire, *Attention Media Group* • *Denver, Colorado*

Cover Dogs:
    Angus Shannon/DeVries and Pepper House

Front cover photographs & story digital photo composites:
    Ardeth De Vries

Back cover original watercolor illustration:
    Ellaine Shannon

Published by:
    PublishingWorks
    60 Winter Street
    Exeter, New Hampshire 03833
    800/333-9883
    www.publishingworks.com

ISBN: 1-933002-29-8

LCN: 2006

Beyond any sense of space and time there is Ellaine. Now a vivid memory of **dazzling** colors and *soft* light, shining through every page of this book.

Even though she's gone on to her next expression of spirit, she continues to touch the hearts of both animals and humans in a way that is profoundly simple, yet complex and intriguing.

Ever present through the light of her art and her loving respect for animals is her gentle spirit and the absolute truth of her wisdom:

WE ARE, INDEED, ALL ONE.

First Light: that moment of clarity when all is revealed, and we know with absolute certainty that we are all one.

This book is dedicated to the animal messengers of this world.

They are always willing and able to provide *first light* experiences for humans.

We simply need to listen.

Acknowledgments

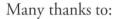

Many thanks to:

🐾 the animals featured in this book for encouraging me to tell their stories and for welcoming me as a friend.

🐾 my dear little boy, Cooper: an extraordinary dog that deserves a story, but it isn't included here because it's too painful to tell and too sad to read.

🐾 the humans who have shared their animal friends with me, and who have either permitted me to photograph their dogs, or who have provided favorite pictures of their own to be used in the stories: Kit and Mark Lathrop, Bill Applegate and family, Barb and Ron Murphy, Popcorn Park, the Matlock family, Doreen and Tank Lucas, Kevin and Torii Locke, Ron Kerrigan, Maureen Martin, John McDonough, Shari and Nick Bibich, Ellen and Ray Bond, Renee and Wes Hammer, Holly French, Harry's dad, Joyce King, Joanne and Clark Craig, Beverly, Jean and Bud Skinner, Mary and Hal Todd, Printon Pollock, Barb and Rick Gliniak, Barb and Curt Bland, Diana Griffin, Whidbey Animals' Improvement Foundation, Donna Keeler, and the Miranda family.

🐾 the many people who have read these stories and offered valuable suggestions and comments.

🐾 Doug Schafer for teaching me the difference between a pixel and a peanut butter sandwich.

🐾 Mark Cannelora, grammarian extraordinaire.

🐾 Medley Cannelora, Peggy Claire, and Penny Holland for their skilled editing and eagle-eye proofreading.

🐾 Grant Dunmire at Attention Media Group for his expertise and imaginative wizardry.

🐾 Jeremy Townsend at J.N. Townsend Publishing & Publishing Works for her animal heart.

🐾 Peggy Claire for her imaginative and comprehensive PR efforts; she's made it possible for the animal voices in *First Light* to be heard by everyone on this beautiful island.

🐾 Ellaine for her love, encouragement and forty years of *first light* experiences.

Table of Contents

Preface

It is my hope that you will be inspired, touched, amused, educated, and even outraged as you read the stories in *FIRST LIGHT*. The animals are real and the stories are inspired by actual events.

More importantly, I want you to be moved to action by this book. There is much to be done to promote animal welfare, and there are many issues addressed in this collection of stories that deserve attention by humans.

If the animals you meet in *FIRST LIGHT* touch your heart, then I hope that you'll take action in at least one of the following ways:

- 🐾 volunteer at your local animal shelter,
- 🐾 adopt a dog or cat from a shelter,
- 🐾 write letters to ban Greyhound racing,
- 🐾 involve your animal friends in the dying process of family members,
- 🐾 play on the beach with your companion animals,
- 🐾 relentlessly pursue authorities to remove animals from places of neglect and abuse,
- 🐾 actively work to change laws and county ordinances regarding animal welfare,
- 🐾 contact Popcorn Park Zoo (www.popcornpark.org) to find out how you can sponsor an animal,
- 🐾 teach children to be kind to animals,
- 🐾 make arrangements for the care and well-being of your companion animals in case of illness or death,
- 🐾 contribute what you can to organizations that promote animal welfare,
- 🐾 and finally, I hope that you'll allow your animal friends to provide *first light* experiences for you.

If you're willing to take action in any of the areas listed above, I promise you that your life will be changed forever, and you **will** know with absolute certainty that we are all one.

FIRST LIGHT is not a treatise on interspecies communication; it is simply my journey with the animals I love. Allowing the animals to engage in dialogue is not an attempt to endorse anthropomorphism, but rather it is merely a literary device that permits you to hear their voices and learn from them. Animals have no need for words when they communicate; unfortunately, humans tend to rely on them to a far greater degree than necessary. Just as Richard Bach delivered an "uncommon treat" by permitting Jonathan Livingston Seagull to tell his story, I hope that my animal friends will present a similar gift to you.

You should know too, that any royalties earned by me from this book will be donated to animal welfare organizations. Let's hear it for the animals!

Ardeth De Vries
September 2005

Zippetydoodah

Zippy danced circles around the little red-haired boy as they made their way to the bus stop. Every so often the leash would get tangled up in the boy's legs, and he would stop and try to unwind it while Zippy did his imitation of a whirling dervish. When the two became hopelessly tangled, the father would stop pushing the baby carriage long enough to lend assistance. It was hard to tell which sound was the happier, the boy's laughter or Zippy's barking. And so it went, this funny parade of dad, baby, boy and dog, all going to the bus stop so the boy could catch the school bus.

As I watched the action from my deck, I could see others arriving at the bus shelter. Zippy and his entourage made their entrance as four Pugs pulled a woman to a screeching halt right in front of them. Freddie, Timmy, Charlie and Jimmy strained at their leashes trying to get close enough to Zippy to say hello. Zippy did his dance, and soon everyone was tangled in leashes. I could hear laughing as the humans tried to figure out how to get the dogs unsnarled. Four fat Pugs and a Jack Russell Terrier swirling around each other while adults and kids couldn't figure out what to do was a pretty funny sight.

"Hey, Zippy." "What's up?" "How ya doin'?" "C'mon over closer and say hi."

"Hi, everybody. Great day, isn't it? "

The humans finally figured out that if they stood still, the dogs could greet each other and everything would be fine. Dogs checked each other out, chased around as much as they could, and generally did their socializing while the red-haired boy greeted the girl who came with the Pugs. The adults said their good mornings too, and all was quiet for a minute.

Then the next group arrived. Mocha, a young chocolate Lab, enthusiastically wagged her tail as she ran up to Zippy and the gang. The little girl who'd arrived with Mocha dropped her leash and went over to greet her friends while her mom stood by and smiled. What a picture! Mocha hopped around, trying not to step on the five small dogs as they raced around her legs. Finally Mocha gave up trying to play in a standing position and sat down. The little guys tumbled all over her, and she grinned happily. All tails were wagging like furry windshield wipers in the fast mode.

By this time, the adults had relinquished the leashes. No problem. The dogs weren't interested in going anywhere. Why wander off when you could have so much fun where you were?

"Hey kids, here comes the bus."

With those magic words, all action stopped, adults grabbed leashes, and the dogs sorted themselves out as the big yellow bus pulled up. The children climbed aboard, dogs sat calmly, the bus pulled away, and adults and dogs went their separate ways.

As I watched the dogs and their people move off in different directions, I couldn't help but smile as I thought about the joys of living in a small town. In my little island village, dogs and grown-ups walk their children to the bus in the morning. I get to watch this ritual almost every day, and each day I count my blessings and am so happy to see animals and people interact in such a wonderful way. In this town, folks even slow their cars on Main Street so the deer can walk freely across the street. As it should be.

As I stood on the deck, I thought about Zippy. I knew the other dogs pretty well, but he was new to the neighborhood and I knew his name only because I could hear his little boy calling him from time to time. Whenever I saw him, I was reminded of another Jack Russell I had known who even had the same name. Probably a pretty common name for such an energetic little dog.

I'd never had the opportunity to get to know the other terrier very well and I wondered what this Zippy's life was like when he wasn't at the bus stop. I could see that he was a happy little guy, and I had a strong urge to spend some time with him. I wondered how to do that. Could I go to his house (I knew where he lived), go up to the door and say something like, "May Zippy come out and play?"

Why not? What could happen? People in the neighborhood know that I'm an animal person, and if I want to take Zippy for a walk, what harm could there be in that? Maybe his family is busy or gone during the day and would appreciate someone spending time with the dog. Maybe they'll think my request is odd, but so what?

The next day I was at the bus stop too. I hung around with a cup of coffee in my hand, just like the other adults, and I went around and introduced myself to those who didn't know me. I told them that I'd been watching the action and couldn't resist coming down and getting a closer look. After the bus came and the group broke up, I walked with Zippy's person and a perfect opportunity came up for my offer when he said that Zippy loved the morning outing. He added that he felt badly because he and his wife didn't have time to take him out more often. Perfect. I said that I had time during the day and offered to come by and walk him now and then if he didn't mind.

Not only did he not mind, he was delighted that Zippy could get some exercise during the day. Both he and his wife worked, the baby went to day care, the little boy was in school, and Zippy was alone until they came home from work. By the time we arrived at his house, I'd set up a walking schedule for Zippy. The man didn't know that I was more interested in talking to Zippy than walking him, but Zippy did. All the time we'd been walking, Zippy kept looking at me, and when I bent down to say goodbye to him before I left, he gave me a quick slurp and said, "See you soon, Dale."

I didn't question the fact that Zippy knew my name. Long ago I'd come to believe that dogs know most everything there is to know about people. They just do. The fact that most people don't understand this speaks volumes about what humans don't know about animals.

When I went to Zippy's house to get him a couple of days later, he was ready to go. In fact, he was raring to go! After we said our hellos in the house, he showed me where his leash was hanging and we took off down the street.

"Zippy, my friend, what do you need to know about me? I know we don't know each other."

"Oh, I know you. I've seen you watching us from your house. I wondered how long it would take you to come and meet us. Besides, you knew my brother. I know you remember him."

"Your brother? Did he live around here? I don't usually forget dogs I've met before."

"No. You didn't meet him in the neighborhood. You met him at the animal shelter. You took him for walks and played with him."

By this time, we were down near the wharf and I'd stopped to sit on the bench near the pier. Zippy jumped up on my lap and looked at me intently as he waited for me to remember his brother.

I held his face in my hands and couldn't believe that I'd been so slow to understand the obvious. "Zippy! Of course I knew your brother. I get it now. You look exactly like him. I think of him every time I see you. You even have the same name. How's that possible?" I was babbling, and Zippy sat there calmly waiting for me to run down.

"Anything's possible, Dale. There were two of us, and we each got adopted by different people. We ended up with the same name because, well, I guess because we're zippy kinda guys."

Now it all came back to me. The Zippy I knew was the cute little eight month old Jack Russell Terrier who had ended up at the shelter because he'd been given as a gift to someone who not only hadn't asked for a dog, but didn't want one. The man to whom he'd been given had lost his wife, and his children had decided that he needed a dog so they bought Zippy from a breeder and presented him to their father. Zippy was a puppy that needed love and attention, neither of which the man was able to give because he was still grieving for his wife. That's how Zippy became homeless.

"Zippy. Dear Zippy. I remember your brother so well. I've thought about him often. The first time I saw you at the bus stop, you reminded me so much of him. I guess that's why I wanted to meet you."

"I've wanted to meet you too. I figured we'd catch up with each other eventually. You gotta know my brother is fine. And me? I'm having lots of fun. I have a kid and a baby who play with me, and I get to be in the house and even sleep with my boy. The adults in this family want me too. They aren't like my brother's human who didn't like him or have time for him. I've got a family who loves me. It's great. C'mon, let's walk some more."

I had more questions, but I figured they could wait so I stood up and we continued our walk. We wandered through town and since it was a warm spring day, I asked Zippy if he'd like to share an ice cream cone. (The kind I had in mind was a special non-dairy-dog-friendly cone, but I was sure he wouldn't care what kind of cone we shared, so I didn't bother to tell him. I figured he'd enjoy it more if he thought he was eating something that generally appeared on the "10 Most Wanted List of Foods You Never Feed a Dog.")

"Are you kidding? You bet! I want the kind with chocolate and nuts. Oh, and maybe some marshmallow stuff on it. And, maybe some chewy stuff inside. And … "

"Okay, okay, I get the picture. But, I'm not getting you any chocolate or nuts or marshmallow or any gooey stuff. That kind is called Rocky Road, and you'll be rocky all right if you eat that. You'll get sick. You know that."

"Well, I guess you're right. No harm in trying. How about the white kind? And make it a double so we both have enough."

I tied Zippy to the bench outside of the ice cream parlor and went in to get our cone. He told me to hurry because he was starving (not likely). After I came out of the store, I joined Zippy at the bench. He hopped up, and I soon found out that his version of sharing was that he bit great hunks of ice cream, while I tried to get a lick in now and then.

"You're supposed to lick the cone, kiddo. Not take big bites. There's enough for both of us."

"I know, I know. We have to hurry and that's why I'm eating fast."

"What's the rush? We just got here. It's a beautiful day. Relax."

"Right, but we're needed in the park, and we won't get there in time if we stay here too long."

"Needed? In the park?"

"C'mon Dale, you don't have to repeat everything. You heard me. We have to go to the park because there's a bird in trouble there, and we have to help her."

Once again, I knew better than to question, so we quickly finished our cone and took off toward the park. It was only a block away and with Zippy pulling me along we made it in record time. When we got to the park, I looked around to see if I could find a bird in trouble, but I needn't have bothered because Zippy dragged me to a spot under one of the hemlock trees that line the park on the water side. There, on the ground, was what appeared to be a cockatiel. I don't know much about birds, but I knew that this bird wasn't a typical outside bird. She was very quiet and didn't seem to be breathing.

"Pick her up, Dale, and breathe into her mouth. She's stunned because she flew into the tree and knocked herself out. You have to revive her."

I hadn't ever performed CPR on a bird, but I did what Zippy told me to do, and soon my efforts were rewarded by a feeble struggle and a slight flapping of wings.

"Hi. Thanks for helping me. I was lost, hit the tree and blacked out. I'll be okay. Just give me a minute."

I sat on the ground under the tree with Zippy at my side and the bird cradled in my hands, while I gently stroked her back. Zippy even toned down some of his exuberance to sit quietly until her breathing became less ragged and she was able to manage a wobbly standing position in the palms of my hands.

"That's better. I'm fine, now. You can set me down."

I gently set her down on the ground and watched as she took a few hesitant steps. She was still shaky, but she ruffled her feathers, shook her head, and was downright frisky in a minute or so. She looked at both of us and quickly hopped up on Zippy's head.

Amazingly enough, this little ball of dog energy sat quietly while the bird sat on his head. What a cute sight.

"All right, little one, what's your name and how did you get here?"

"My name is Piper and I live in the little store over there near the pier. My human friend understands that I don't like being in a cage and so I was sitting on my perch outside of the cage as usual. Somebody came along, picked me up and carried me out of the store. It all happened so fast, I didn't know what to do, and my friend didn't see it happen because she was waiting on a customer. Whoever it was stuffed me in a pocket, and I bounced around in the pocket until I was let go. I haven't been outside much, so I didn't know where I was at first. I was pretty scared, but I figured if I could get up higher I could see better and maybe find my way back to the store. I took off, but I wasn't watching where I was going, and I banged into a tree."

"Amazing. That's an awful story. What a terrible experience for you. Why don't we take you back to your friend? She must be worried about you."

"Oh, would you, please? I'm feeling much better now, but I can ride on Zippy until we get there. I don't think it's far."

The bird knew the dog's name. My, my …

I knew the store where Piper lived, so the three of us started walking back to the little shop, Zippy moving as sedately as he could with the bird bouncing along on his head.

I couldn't help but tease Zippy. "Hey, Zip. You look pretty cute. Ever walk with a bird on your head before? I didn't think you could walk so slowly."

"All right, all right, Dale; gimme a break. I've got a job to do here. If Piper wants to ride on my head, she gets to ride on my head. It's no big deal. I just hope nobody sees us. I feel sorta silly. Do I look dumb?"

"No, you don't look dumb. The two of you look pretty cute. Don't worry about anyone seeing you. We're almost at the store and there's nobody around." I didn't tell him that I really wished there was someone to see them. He probably wouldn't have been amused.

We finally arrived at the shop, and I had no sooner opened the door than a woman came rushing over to greet us.

"Piper! Piper! Thank God you're safe. I was so worried about you. I've been looking everywhere. Are you all right? Where did you go?" The woman scooped Piper up in both hands and held the bird next to her face as she made happy sounds and stroked Piper's back.

"I think she's fine. We found her in the park. She had the wind knocked out of her."

"Yeah, and she rode the whole way here on top of my head. She's a neat bird. I like her. I walked real slow so she wouldn't tip over."

The woman didn't seem to hear Zippy, but she turned to me. She was incredulous. "In the park? How did she get there?"

"I think someone took her from your store and then let her go in the park. She was frightened and tried to fly up into the tree so she could see where she was, but she hit the tree and knocked herself out. We found her on the ground, revived her and brought her back here."

"I feel terrible. I never saw anything happen. I was waiting on someone, and then I was busy stocking shelves. When I went over to Piper's perch a little later, she was gone. I thought she was still in the store somewhere, but I looked everywhere and couldn't find her. I even went upstairs to look in our apartment, but she wasn't there either. I never thought she'd be outside because I couldn't imagine how she could get out. I've been frantic because I couldn't figure out what happened to her. Thank you so much for bringing her back."

By this time, the woman had placed Piper back on her perch and the bird was busy grooming herself, acting as though nothing had happened. Zippy was sniffing around the store, but there didn't seem to be much to interest him since it was a place that had all kinds of supplies for birds and not dogs. There wasn't an ice cream cone or a dog cookie in sight.

The woman was busy fussing over Piper and she seemed reassured that all was well. After a bit, she turned to me and said, "I'm so glad you happened to be in the park. If you hadn't found her, I don't know what would have happened. Your dog is so cute to let her ride on his head. She likes to do that, but I've never seen her do it with a dog before."

I started to tell her that Zippy wasn't my dog, and that we hadn't just happened to be in the park, but as I began talking, Zippy grabbed his leash and made for the door. Clearly, he didn't want me to tell her about his knowing the bird was in trouble, so I told her that we were happy to help, and went over to say goodbye to Piper before we left.

"Bye, Piper. It was a pleasure to meet you. We'll stop by and see you again, now that we know where you are."

"Bye, Dale. (She knew my name too. I love it.) Bye, Zippy. Thanks for hearing me and coming to my rescue. You're pretty neat … for a dog."

Zippy gave her a big grin and pulled me toward the door. Obviously, it was time to go. The woman walked us out, patting my arm the whole time, continuing to thank me, wondering out loud how I knew that someone had taken Piper. I wanted to tell her that she was thanking the wrong one, and that it was Zippy who knew she'd been taken, but I just smiled and we went on our way.

Once out of the store, we walked down to the water's edge and I pulled Zippy up close.

"Okay, my friend. Do you want to tell me what that was all about? How did you know there was a bird in trouble in the park?"

"What do you mean, how did I know? I felt it. She said she needed help, and I heard her. What's the big deal?"

"The big deal, my little hero, is that you heard her. I didn't hear her. Why didn't I hear her?"

"I dunno, Dale. Maybe you weren't listening. Humans don't always listen to what there is to hear. You guys aren't tuned in sometimes. You have too many words in your heads and you miss stuff. Hey, look at that starfish! Isn't she pretty?"

"Come back here, you rascal. Don't change the subject. Yes, the starfish is beautiful, but I want you to tell me how I can hear like you do."

By now, Zippy was paddling around in the water, poking his nose at the starfish. I pulled him back to me and sat down with him on my lap. He was all wet, and he squirmed around, trying to get back to the object of his interest. Our conversation was evidently boring him.

"Look, Dale, hearing or knowing what another living being is feeling isn't hard. You have to open your heart. You do it all the time and don't even know you're doing it. There's nothing to explain. Let's walk some more."

"Okay, I guess we'd better head back to your house. We've been gone quite awhile, and I don't want your people to come home and worry about you. I promised that I'd have you back by the time they got home from work."

Reluctantly, we made our way back to Zippy's house. He was a wonderful walking companion because he was interested in everything. And his energy was amazing! He smelled every bush, checked his P-mail, and I don't think he missed seeing anything. I had so many questions, but each time I started to talk, he shook his head and said, "Not now, Dale. Just enjoy the walk." I had a hard time keeping up with him, and by the time we arrived back at his house, I felt like I'd run a marathon. I let him in, unhooked his leash, made sure he had enough water, gave him a hug, and told him I'd see him again in a few days.

That day was the beginning of my adventures with Zippy. He and I walk a couple of times a week now, and each walk, although not as eventful as the first, is a wonderful learning experience for me. He answers all of my questions, and he's as patient with me as a terrier can be. Now all I have to do is process everything he tells me and make it work in my life. Always encouraging, he says I'm getting better. He's teaching me to listen with my heart.

The bottom line in terms of what he's teaching me is one of those simple but not easy lessons.

We're all one.

All life is connected.

That's it.

Zippetydoodah! Ain't life grand?

Farm Dogs

Before I met Easy and Sheba, I was convinced that all dogs should sleep in the house every night. On the bed … maybe even under the covers on cold nights. I was absolutely certain that any human who allowed a dog to be outside for any length of time, without being confined in a securely fenced yard, was negligent and uncaring.

Then I met Sheba and Easy.

When I drive to the beach with the dogs every morning I pass a large working farm. The primary crop is strawberries, but the Beech family also grows many different kinds of vegetables as well as flowers whose seeds are sold as crops. They raise sheep to harvest their wool, and they keep cows whose milk is sold. Only a small portion of the farm can be seen from the road, and until last week I had no idea how large the farm actually is in terms of acres. The only part of the farm that I can see from the road is usually planted in strawberries and that facet of the farming process caused me to stop one morning last week.

As I approached the Beech farm, I saw four ladies sitting in a flat bed truck, their legs dangling off the back. The truck moved slowly as the ladies dropped what appeared to be small plants to the ground. It was a warm spring morning, and the women wore bonnets and scarves to shield their faces from the sun. The driver of the flat bed was an older gentleman wearing traditional bib overalls and a long sleeved flannel shirt. Walking behind the truck were two dogs. One was a Border Collie mix, and the other, an Australian Cattle Dog mix. The dogs walked carefully and purposefully in the planting grooves, and they seemed to be scuffling the dirt with their feet every once in a while, but I was too far away to really see what they were doing. Whatever it was, the ladies approved and no one told them to move away.

Because I was fascinated with the process, I stopped the car and watched for a bit. I could see the truck reach the end of a row and then turn and head back in my direction. Curious to see if what I thought I was seeing was actually happening, I got out of the car and went over to the fence that borders the field. As I stood there watching the truck, the planting group pulled up right in front of me and stopped. The driver smiled and asked if he could help me.

"No, I'm fine. I didn't mean to interrupt your work, but I'm curious about what you're doing. Are you planting strawberries?"

"Sure are. Perfect day for it, isn't it girls?"

The "girls," who were anything but, smiled and agreed that indeed the day was beautiful. Now that they were close to me, I could see that all four women were tanned and healthy. These were older women who looked as if they'd been doing this for years. Behind each of them on the flat bed was a large box containing the small plants they were dropping to the ground.

The woman sitting closest to me reached around the box of plants behind her and pulled out a large thermos. "It's time for some coffee. Why don't you join us?"

"I'd love to, but I don't want to intrude. I just wanted to watch what you were doing."

"Don't be silly. You can't see anything from out there. Drive your car into the driveway and walk back here. We can tell you more about what we're doing if you'd like."

I told her that I'd love to learn more and did as she instructed. After I parked the car and started walking back to the group, who by now were all drinking coffee, the two dogs joined me and escorted me back to the truck.

"Hi guys. I'm Dale. Who're you?"

The Border Collie told me that his name was Easy and the Australian Cattle Dog said that she was called Sheba. I wanted to talk more, but we'd barely had time for our introductions before we were back at the truck and one of the ladies handed me a cup of coffee in a well-used tin cup. I thanked her and introduced myself.

The driver held out his hand and said that he was Wes Beech. He then pointed to the ladies and introduced them, one by one. "This is Belle, my wife. Next to her are my sisters, Lucy and Eva. Sitting next to Eva is Alice, my sister-in-law. I can see that you've met Easy and Sheba. We're all family here. So, what can we tell you about what we're doing? Seems pretty obvious to me, but then I've done this for years and I'm not looking at us through a fence."

"Well, now that I'm closer, I can see that you're planting strawberries. It looks like hard work to do it this way. Couldn't you use a machine to plant instead of doing it by hand?"

Belle answered this time. "Sure, if we had a machine. Planting machines cost money and this is a small operation, so we do it ourselves. After we finish dropping the bare root plants, then we come back and dig them in. Goes pretty fast with four of us."

"Okay, I understand. But, I'm curious about the dogs. They looked like they were walking very purposefully behind you. What were they doing?"

Lucy laughed and looked affectionately at Easy and Sheba. "These guys are helping. They've been out here with us since they were pups and once they got the hang of what we were doing, they decided that their job was to make sure all the plants were in a row after we dropped them. After all these years our aim is pretty good, but every once in a while one lands outside of the furrow and the dogs kick it back in line with the other plants. We call the dogs our "straightener-uppers.""

Easy and Sheba had flopped down on the ground near Lucy and when they heard her talking about them, they both grinned and nudged her knee with their noses. She tousled the tops of their heads and reached back to fill a bowl with water for them.

We talked for a while longer before the planting crew said that they needed to get back to work, so I thanked them for the coffee, the planting lesson, and said that I had to be on my way too. I didn't have our dogs with me because I was on my way to visit a friend who lives near the Beech farm and I should have been there an hour ago. Wes told me that I was welcome to come back any time, but they'd put me to work if I stayed too long. I told him that I'd be happy to help if they needed an extra hand; I liked these people and wanted to spend more time with them. I especially wanted to get to know Easy and Sheba. Before I knew it, I'd agreed to come back the next day and help them finish the planting process.

The next day … and the next. I spent almost a week at the Beech farm helping them with their planting. In return, they answered all of my city girl questions and proudly showed me every inch of the farm. Easy and Sheba told me all about a dog's life on a farm, which was really why I was there.

The dogs explained that they'd lived with the Beech family ever since Wes had adopted them four years ago from the local shelter. They'd come from different litters, of course, but they assured me that they were brother and sister in the most important way.

"We kind of take care of each other." Easy was just barely the older of the two, but he was clearly the big brother and Sheba deferred to him most of the time. "We have lots of responsibilities, so we have to watch out for each other and help get the jobs done."

"What kind of jobs do you two have to do?" I asked this as we were walking in the field where the sheep were grazing. There were several young lambs that stayed close to their mothers as they all nibbled in the field. I remembered driving by and seeing the lambs not long after they'd been allowed out of the birthing shed; just after they were born, the babies all wore blue, yellow and red sweaters. Now that they were older they didn't need the sweaters any longer because the weather had warmed up and they were perfectly comfortable.

Sheba answered this time. "Well, take these guys here. We have to make sure they all stay where they're supposed to be. And when the lambs are born, we have to watch out for coyotes so the little guys don't get killed. Same with the calves and cows. We watch to be sure they're all safe and if something happens to any of them, we run to get Wes so he can help them. He's got too much to do to watch out for the cows and sheep all the time. He calls us his 'extra eyes'."

Easy was watching the sheep, but he looked away for a minute to add a comment. "Yeah, and we have to make sure that the chickens don't wander off, and we have to help with planting like you saw. We like to pick the strawberries too, but Belle says we eat too many and get sick so we don't do that too much. The squash is pretty good though. They give some to the cows to make sweeter milk and we sneak a few now and then too.

"I guess you guys are farm hands, right? Seems like you have lots to do here. What do you do for fun?"

Sheba grinned. "It's all fun, Dale. This is a great place to live. Oh, yeah, and we get to ride in the truck when Wes runs errands and that's fun too."

"He doesn't put you in the back of the truck does he?" Alarm bells were going off in my head about the danger involved in this reckless kind of activity that I see all too often, but Easy was quick to assure me that I needn't worry.

"Oh, no, that's too dangerous. We get to ride in back if he's driving around the farm, but when we go to town with him, we ride up front on the seat."

By now we were heading toward the barn and the dogs raced ahead of me, yelling back at me to hurry up so I could meet Putz.

Putz? I thought I'd met all of the humans and animals here, but no one had said anything about Putz. "Hey, wait up. Who's Putz?"

Easy and Sheba were waiting for me at the side door of the barn and when I arrived, they moved inside and went over to a corner stall. Both of them went into the stall and nudged a small body that was sleeping on a nest of hay. As I moved closer, my nose told me that Putz was a pig. Not a big pig, but a baby pot bellied pig that was blissfully snoring, trying to stay asleep while Easy and Sheba poked at him with their noses.

"I didn't know you had pigs here. Where did he come from? He's just a baby."

Putz was awake and started to squeal as Easy answered my question. "We don't have pigs. Wes found him out in the back forty the other day. He was all alone and starving. Somebody must have dumped him there, so Wes brought him to the barn and he lives here now. At least until we can find a home for him. So, we gotta take care of him too. He'll be okay. He just needs to grow up and get bigger."

As Easy was explaining all of this to me, Putz nuzzled close to him and gave little happy squeals. He knew that the dogs were his friends and he was glad to see them.

"Hi Putz. You're sure a cute little guy." I bent down to give him a hug.

When Putz heard me talking to him he scooted closer and allowed me to pick him up.

"Hi. Hugs. Warm. Nice lady smell. Got food?"

"No, Putz. I don't have any food, but I can get you some if the guys will tell me where to find it."

I was ready to give him whatever he wanted, but Sheba explained that Wes would be along to feed him pretty soon. Easy added that Putz was on a special feeding schedule because he was a baby and he ate small amounts several times a day. So, I deferred to their expertise and put Putz back down in his nest of hay and, after he squirmed around a bit, he went to sleep again.

After we left Putz and were walking back to the side door of the barn, Easy and Sheba stopped to get drinks from two water bowls that were standing near the door. I also noticed that there were two blankets near the bowls. "This isn't where you sleep, is it? You don't have to actually sleep in the barn, do you?"

Sheba smiled because she knew what I was thinking. "No, Dale, we don't have to sleep in the barn. Sometimes we do though, to keep an eye on things. Lots of times we sleep here because it's nice. There are great smells and it's cool on warm summer evenings. In the winter, if it's cold, we're welcome in the house. Matter of fact, we're welcome anywhere on the farm. We get to be wherever we want to be."

I got the message. I was quickly learning that some of my rigid standards about dog necessities weren't applicable to all dogs in every situation. Guess it's never too late to learn.

As we continued our walk, I noticed that Wes was working on an old tractor that had seen better days. He waved and motioned for us to join him. "I see that you're coming from the barn so you must have met Putz. I need to get over and feed him pretty soon. Are you on your way to see the horses?"

"You'll have to ask my tour guides. The guys have been showing me around and I follow them." As I said this, I looked over at the dogs to see if we were going to see the horses, but they were already heading toward the small pasture I could see in the distance. "Yeah, I guess we are. Is there anything I can help you with here?" I had no idea how to fix a tractor, but I figured I could hand him tools or do something to be of help.

"Nope. This old tractor is giving me fits again, but I'll get her running. She's old, but still works most of the time." He reached in his back pocket and pulled out a couple of carrots. "Here. Give these to Trula and Fancy Boy. I was on my way over there, but I got sidetracked with the tractor."

I took the carrots and told him I'd see him later as I ran to catch up with the dogs. By the time I got to the pasture, Easy and Sheba had already scooted under the fence rails and were playing their own version of tag between two horses that were patiently standing there watching them. As I walked toward the horses, both of them came right over to me, intent on the carrots in my hand.

"Hi you two; I guess these are yours. Wes said for me to give them to you. I know that your names are Trula and Fancy Boy, but I don't know …"

Before I could finish my sentence, Easy came sliding to a stop in front of the chestnut colored horse that was happily munching on a carrot. "This is Trula, and the shiny dark guy is Fancy Boy. They're pretty neat…for horses. They were here even before we came. Trula is Fancy Boy's mom."

I introduced myself to the two beautiful animals and ran my hands along their sleek necks. They both looked healthy and they seemed very content. "What do you two beauties do here? What's your life like?"

Trula was still munching, so Fancy Boy answered me. "Well, we hang out in the pasture most of the time. Sometimes the kids from town come out and we pull the wagon for hay rides. Everybody in the family likes to ride us; we get to take them all around when they want to explore and see what's happening in the back forty or on the other side of the farm. We work too, pulling the wagon when it's time to harvest the squash. Wes's tractor doesn't always run and we're happy to be his tractor if he needs us. It's a great life."

I was ready to ask more questions, but I looked around for the dogs and couldn't see them anywhere. One minute they were playing tag, and then they were gone. Trula saw the worried expression on my face and reassured me about Easy and Sheba. "Don't worry about those guys. They're probably off playing with the dogs across the road. Head over there and you'll probably see them."

I didn't like the idea of the dogs being near the road, so I quickly thanked Trula, told both horses that it was nice to meet them and walked toward the front part of the farm that borders the road. Sure enough, I could see Easy and Sheba playing with two other dogs. I walked over and joined them.

"Are you sure you guys should be here? What if a car comes along and you get hit? I've seen too many animals get hit on this road. It's dangerous for you to wander around like this. Aren't you supposed to stay on the farm?" I knew that I must sound like a warden, but I wasn't used to seeing dogs outside of a fenced yard unless it was at the beach.

Easy and Sheba said goodbye to their friends, both yellow Labs, and walked back to the Beech farm with me. When we got to the strawberry field, which was now beautifully planted, we stopped and Easy answered my questions.

"Relax, Dale. We're fine. We visit Suze and Rambo all the time. We won't get hit by a car."

"I know you say that Easy, but I've seen dogs get hit on this road. What makes you so sure that it won't be you or Sheba some day?"

"I know that it won't happen to us because we know we're loved where we live and when we cross the road, we're not running away. We're not scared, hungry, or lonely. That's what's going on with the dogs that you see getting hit. There was a dog a couple of farms down that was killed awhile back because he was running away and wasn't paying attention. He didn't have a good life like we do. He didn't have any reason to stay around the farm because nobody ever paid any attention to him. The people kept him chained up all the time and so first chance he got, he broke the chain and ran. He wasn't part of the family."

"So, are you saying that people don't need to keep their dogs in a fenced yard? Ever? I have a hard time with that idea. It doesn't seem responsible to me."

Sheba spoke up this time. "No, Dale, that's not what Easy is saying. Depends on lots of things. We have a special relationship with our humans here. We don't want to be anywhere else. We're connected to everything that happens here. When we cross the road, we always look to be sure it's safe. No matter where we are, we always still feel like we're attached to our people. We don't stay away for long. And when we know we're going over to see our friends, we always let Wes or one of the ladies know where we're going. When we passed Wes on our way over, we told him we were off to see Suze and Rambo. Our humans always tell us where they're going when they leave the farm and we do the same for them. Like Wes told you, we're family here."

Easy added, "Yeah, and it depends too on where you live. Running around in a city or town could be dangerous, even if you watched where you were going. City and town dogs should always be kept safe in a fenced yard."

"Okay, I get the picture. I guess I'm trying to apply general ideas to every situation, and you've both taught me that it doesn't always work that way. Being on the farm this week has been a real eye-opener for me in more ways than one. Thanks."

As much as I was enjoying my new friends, it really was time for me to leave. I walked back to Wes and thanked him for the wonderful time I'd had during the week, and then went into the house to say goodbye to the ladies who were getting canning supplies ready for the summer. I promised I'd come back and visit often, and they in turn said they'd stop and see me when they were in town.

Easy and Sheba walked me to my car and gave me great kisses as I hugged them both and said goodbye. I told them that I'd probably be back in June when the strawberries were ready to be picked and they both offered to help.

"No thanks. You'd probably eat most of what I picked. I'll settle for the pleasure of your company when I do come back."

I got in the car and was about to say goodbye again when I heard Wes's voice. "Easy! Sheba! I need you two. Sheep are out and I need your help!"

Before I could even turn my head, the dogs were off. I could hear them shouting instructions to each other as they ran. Watching them go, I knew that the sheep would be rounded up before they even knew they were out. As I started to leave, a mental picture quickly formed in my head. I imagined Easy and Sheba teaching Putz how to round up sheep and cattle. I wonder if Hollywood is ready for another movie about a sheep herding pig. Watch out, Babe!

On Being a Shelter Dog

Uh oh, here comes another one. I wonder if he's a stray like me, or maybe his people had to move and didn't take him with them to their new home. Never could understand this business of adopting a dog and then giving the dog up because it isn't convenient to take him with the family to a new place.

Humans are so funny. They don't do that with their children, but somehow dogs aren't important enough I guess. They don't get that we have feelings too and when we end up in an animal shelter, it's hard on us.

There are people here who try to make us feel loved and comfortable, but no matter how you cut it, living in a cage is the pits.

"Hey, new guy. Are you okay? I know you can't see me, but if you can settle down, you'll be able to hear me talking to you. Not words, like people use, but heart-talk. I'm right next door. Listen up."

"Where am I? It's so noisy here. I'm scared."

"Yeah, I know. I know. Just calm down and you'll be okay. Where're you from? How'd you get here?"

"Man, I'm so tired. I feel like I've been running for days. My people kept me chained up in the backyard, and I couldn't take it anymore. I had to get away, so I kept pulling as hard as I could, and I broke the chain and ran. My neck is so sore I can hardly stand it. But, at least I got out of that place. Somebody in a truck picked me up and brought me here. I'm so hungry. They didn't feed me much and I'm starved."

"Don't worry about that part. Somebody will come in a minute and give you some food and water and you'll feel better. They do that right away. You'll probably get a blanket too, but don't chew on it though; otherwise, you won't get another one."

"A blanket, really? All I had to sleep on was dirt, so no way am I gonna chew on a blanket. I hope it's a soft one. My butt is sore and my legs are killing me."

"It'll be soft, all right. Nice and clean too. So, how come you were chained up in the backyard? Did you do something wrong?"

"I don't know; I tried to be good. I lived with these people ever since I was a puppy, and even when they first got me, they kept me locked up in a small room in the house most of the time. They were gone all day, and then when they came home at night, they took me out and played with me a little bit, but I never felt like I was part of the family. I tried to be a good dog, but I never knew what they wanted from me. The kids were kinda rough with me, but the adults never talked to them about how to treat me. I didn't know what to do about it except to play with the kids and keep away from them when they hit me. Sometimes I'd growl and bark at the kids, trying to tell them to treat me nice, but they didn't get it and if the adults saw me growl at the kids, then they hit me too. It was so frustrating. All I wanted was for them to be kind to me and to love me, but I couldn't get through to them. Then, when I got bigger, they chained me up in the backyard like they didn't want me any more."

"Yeah, I know the feeling. We're all here for kinda the same reason."

"So, what's this place like? What happens now?"

"Well, it's better than being on the run, but it's not an easy place to be because it gets so lonely and there are so many rules. Everybody here is pretty nice, and you get food, water, a blanket, and sometimes people come and take you for a walk. That's the best part. The ones who come and take you for walks are the volunteers. I wish there were more of them because we don't always get out every day. But, you gotta be good and nice to everybody. Oh, and the vet will come and check you out to be sure there's nothing wrong with you. Is your neck okay?"

"Yeah, I guess, but it feels pretty raw, so maybe if the vet comes, he'll put some stuff on it to keep it from hurting. They already checked it out when I came in so I think they know about it. They really looked me over before they brought me back here. Whadda ya mean about the rules?"

"Rules are so they can tell if you're adoptable. Stuff like you can't bark a lot, growl at anybody, and never, never try to bite anybody. That'll get you dead for sure. You've gotta be friendly and nice to people. It's important to tell them what you're like so they can write all kinds of stuff on the little card on your cage so when people come around to adopt a dog, they know about you and will want to take you home with them."

"Okay, I get it. But, how can I let people know what I'm like if I'm stuck in this cage?"

"That's the hard part. You don't usually get to spend a lot of time with any one person, so you have to be nice to everybody who comes around so they all have the same ideas about you. If everyone thinks you're a great dog, they'll talk about you and when someone comes to the shelter to adopt a dog, the person taking them around will have good things to say about you. It's a pretty stressful situation, but it's all we have right now and if you want to get out of here, you'd better make the best of it."

"So, if you know all this stuff, how come you're still here?"

"Yeah, well, I know the rules all right, but I'm not good about following them. I'm a kinda hyper guy and so when somebody comes up to my cage, I bark a lot and that scares 'em a little and nobody wants to spend much time with me."

"If you know you're not supposed to bark, how come you still do it?"

"Good question. I guess I've spent so much time being ignored by people that I bark to get noticed, even though it puts people off. I'm probably a little like the kid who will do anything to get attention, even if it's the wrong thing. Sometimes I see somebody who reminds me of the human who didn't treat me right and I bark because I'm scared. Even though I know it's not the same person, I get so scared that I can't help myself."

"I get that, but can't you let people know why you bark so they'll give you attention and it'll be okay?"

"I try, believe me. I try. I don't know what else to do. I guess if I sat here and tried to look cute, it would be better, but I get so anxious and nervous sometimes, it's hard to sit still."

"Yeah, I guess. So, how long have you been here?"

"I dunno. Seems like forever. Oh good, here comes Jeff with some food, water, and a blanket for you. He's a neat guy. Be nice."

"Yeah, I see him. Talk to you later."

"Hey, Andrew. How're you doing today?"

"Oh, hi Dale. I'm okay. Did you meet the new guy next door? He just came in and Jeff's bringing him his food now."

"Yeah, I can see that. Why don't we go for a walk so he has a chance to eat and then I can meet him when we come back."

"Oh, please, it'll be so good to get out of this cage. Let's go to the exercise pen so I can run a little before we walk, okay?"

"You bet. Anything you want, my friend."

Andrew and I went over to the exercise pen and we played ball for about fifteen minutes before we went for our walk. I so wished that I could take him to the beach and let him run. He wasn't handling being at the shelter well at all. About two months ago he was found wandering on the highway and somebody picked him up and brought him to the shelter. No one came to claim him, so he became a resident.

"Andrew, are you getting any better about that crazy barking?" By now we were walking on the trail near the woods.

"Oh, Dale, I try; really I do. I was talking to the new guy about it. Being in a cage makes me crazy. I'm okay once I get out, but I guess I must have the dog version of … claus …what do you humans call it?"

"Claustrophobia. Yeah, I'm sure you do. But it's so hard for people to like you when they're standing in front of your cage and you're barking so loudly. You scare people. You don't do that with me though. Why not?"

"I don't need to bark at you. You hear me when I talk to you and you understand. And, I know that when you come to the front of my cage you're going to take me out."

"But, Andrew, you know that I'm usually here for several hours when I come, and I don't spend all of my time with you. The other guys need walks too. When I walk past your cage to visit with another dog, you don't bark at me then either."

"I know. It's because you always say hi to me when you walk past, and I know you'll take me out one last time before you go home. I know what to expect from you and I know you worry about me and care about me."

"True, I do, but there are other people here who worry and care about you too. You know that. Everyone here wants to see you get adopted and live in a forever home with people who love you. "

"I know, but sometimes I get so crazy with being here that all I can do is just bark. Why won't somebody adopt me and take me out of here? Can't you tell people that I'm good?"

"I do, my friend. I tell everyone what a great dog you are. The problem is that I'm not here all the time and sometimes when I come in, I hear that when people came to look at you, you barked at them and scared them away. I don't know what else to do for you. You gotta get a grip."

We had finished our walk and were now heading back toward the shelter. I felt so frustrated for this wonderful dog. We all hoped that he could hang on until someone was able to see past his barking and give him a chance. Once he was out of the shelter I knew he'd be fine, but so far we hadn't been able to make the right connection for Andrew. People coming to adopt a dog from a shelter aren't always willing to look beyond the obvious; prospective adopters often don't understand that the stress level at a shelter is so high that the dogs are unable to act naturally and are usually very anxious. It's an imperfect system, but at least the dogs are safe and well cared for while they're there, but it's so discouraging that so many, like Andrew, are at the shelter for such a long time.

"Okay, my friend. In you go. I want to meet your new neighbor and then take some of the others out. We'll walk around one last time before I go home. Please try to stay calm. Here's a new chew bone for you. Maybe you can amuse yourself for a while so you won't be so nervous."

After I closed the gate to Andrew's cage, I looked next door and found a big fuzzy dog huddled in the corner. Most of the fur around his neck was missing and the skin was red and raw in places. There was a sign on his cage saying "Staff Only Until Assessed" and so I knew I couldn't take him out yet, but at least I could talk to him and see how he was doing.

"Hi, I'm Dale. What's your name?"

He tentatively walked to the front of the cage and sat down in front of me. "I'm Gus."

"Hi, Gus, welcome. It's nice to meet you. Did you get enough to eat?"

"Yeah, thanks. He filled the bowl really full. It was great."

"Good. You have water and a blanket too?"

"Oh, yeah; the guy next door said I'd get a blanket and he was right. It's a nice big soft one. So, what's up with you? Do you work here?"

"No, I don't work here. I'm a volunteer. I come and walk dogs. As soon as you're able to leave your cage, I'll take you for a walk and we can get to know each other.

"That'd be great. So, do you think I can get adopted pretty soon?"

"I sure hope so. If nobody comes to claim you in five days, then you get to be available. Do you think your people will come and find you?"

"Oh geeze, I hope not! I ran away because I didn't want to be there anymore. I told my story to the guy next door and he knows what's up with me. Will I have to go back to those people if they come to get me?"

"Well, that depends. Maybe they can be convinced to let you stay here so you can go to a better home. We'll have to wait and see. Meanwhile, looks like you could use a rest and some TLC. Somebody will come around pretty soon and assess you and then after that you can go for walks."

"What does this 'assess' mean? What happens?"

"It's okay. Nothing to worry about. Someone will check you out to see how you are with cats, other dogs and with people. They want to be sure that you aren't what they call 'aggressive' and somebody will be able to adopt you."

"Aggressive … that's a weird word. What does it mean?"

"Well, it's a word that humans use to describe dog behavior that isn't acceptable to them- like when a dog growls or tries to bite. They call that being aggressive."

"That's nuts! Don't they understand that when we growl or try to bite that we're trying to tell people we're afraid or need them to be respectful?"

"Some people do, but it's a word that gets used pretty freely around here, so you need to be careful. No one's going to hurt you though. You're safe here."

"Well, everybody I've seen so far has been nice. It's a lot better than where I came from; I'll be okay I think."

The next day Gus was assessed and passed with flying colors; volunteers are able to walk him now and he seems to be doing fine. The vet did come and look at his neck and staff has some ointment they're applying, so the skin is healing nicely. We have to use a harness to walk him since his neck is too raw for a collar, but that isn't a problem for him. He's strong and energetic though and walking him is a real challenge. Once he understands that walking on a leash isn't like being chained up, he should come around.

About a week later I came in and found Andrew even more upset than usual. Not only was he barking non-stop, but he was pacing in his cage like a wild animal.

"Hey, Andrew. Hey, buddy, calm down. Let me get you out of there. Let's go for a walk."

He was almost hysterical and couldn't even talk. Once he was out of his cage, we ran to the exercise area and I let him loose to run. He didn't even take time to talk to me until he'd run around and around for at least ten minutes. Finally, he flopped at my feet.

"Phew … that was as close as I've come to losing it. Thanks for getting me out of there, Dale."

"You're welcome, but what's going on? Why're you so upset?"

"Nothing special I guess, but I can't take being in that cage any more. I'm going nuts. I've gotta get out of here. Don't you know anybody who could take me? I know I'll be all right once I don't have to be in a cage."

"Okay, my friend. Okay. I'll make some calls when I get home and see what we can come up with for you. I know this is very hard for you. In the meantime, let's walk for a bit and then when we come back, I'll cut the grass in here and you can hang out with me until it's time for me to go."

"Great, thanks. I'm feeling better now. Let's hit the trail."

After our walk, I spent the rest of the afternoon cutting the grass in the exercise area while Andrew raced around chasing the lawnmower and burning off some of his excess energy. I knew he couldn't last at the shelter much longer. We absolutely had to find a home for him as soon as possible.

When it was time to put Andrew back in his cage, I gave him a hug and told him to hang on a little while longer. I promised him that I'd call everyone I knew who might be willing to either adopt him or put me in contact with someone else who might offer him a home. I'd done this about a month ago for him, but it was time to make the rounds again. There had to be someone out there who would love this desperate, but wonderful dog.

That night I called a friend who has an older Lab companion and told her about Andrew. I didn't think that she'd be able to take Andrew because three dogs and many cats live with her and her husband, but I thought perhaps she might know of someone who would adopt him. She listened to what I had to say and said she'd get back to me.

About an hour after our conversation, my friend called back and said that she and her husband were willing to give Andrew a chance with them. They weren't sure how their older Lab would respond to him, but they wanted to offer Andrew a home. She said that they hoped Andrew might be a good companion for Swede, their Lab, since they were both about the same size. I told her that it was important for them to bring Swede to meet Andrew at the shelter to see how the two dogs responded to each other. Ideally, it would be better if I could drive Andrew to their home to meet Swede, or if the two dogs could meet on neutral territory, but shelter policy dictated that prospective adopters bring other dogs in the family to the shelter to meet the new dog. She agreed and we arranged for them to meet Andrew the next day.

Tossing and turning replaced sleep for me that night as I thought about Andrew and hoped that he could keep it together when he met Swede and his family. I knew that this had to work; otherwise, the shelter would have to let Andrew go. He couldn't take being there any longer.

The next day I arrived at the shelter about an hour before my friends were scheduled to appear and went out to see Andrew.

"Hey, buddy, guess what? I have someone coming to see you in a little while, and they're bringing one of their dogs to meet you. Let's walk so we can talk about it."

Andrew was so excited he could hardly contain himself. Getting him out of his cage was always a challenge and today it was almost impossible. "Somebody's coming to meet me? Me? Really? Who is it? Can I go home with them? What do I have to do?"

I took Andrew to the exercise area and unleashed him, but instead of doing his usual warp factors around the pen, he wouldn't move until I'd told him about his visitors. "Okay, here's the deal. The people you're going to meet are really nice and they love animals. Three dogs and lots of cats live with them. The two small dogs are Skookie, an American Eskimo, and Shad, a Poodle. Shad and Skookie were adopted from the shelter several years ago. The third dog is Swede, a Lab, like you. They found him in a box in front of Safeway when he was a puppy and he's lived with them his whole life. Swede's an old guy and he's the one you'll meet today."

"You've really got to be on your best behavior today, my friend. I know that these people will love you and take good care of you; your job is to convince them that you won't drive them crazy with your barking and that you'll be a great addition to their family. I know you and I don't need convincing, but they'll be meeting you for the first time. You have to be good. Don't jump on them and don't bark when you see them. Can you do that?"

"You bet. Absolutely. You wait and see; I'll be perfect. They won't be able to resist me."

He **was** perfect and they couldn't resist him. When my friends came, I had them walk down the road that runs past the cages before I brought

Andrew out to meet them. I knew that in spite of his best intentions, Andrew would go nuts if he saw them all standing in front of his cage. My friend and her husband greeted Andrew enthusiastically, but Swede wasn't impressed. Andrew did everything he could to let Swede know that he wouldn't be a threat to his seniority, but Swede wasn't convinced.

The three of us walked with the two dogs for quite a while to see if Swede would come around and accept Andrew. By the time we'd finished our walk, Swede still wasn't overjoyed about Andrew, so I took him aside and talked with him while my friend and her husband walked ahead with Andrew.

"Swede, what is it? Is it seriously going to be a problem for you if Andrew comes to live at your house?"

"I don't know, Dale. He seems nice enough, but I'm the boss there. He sure is hyper. Do you think he'll ever calm down? I'm a pretty quiet guy and I can't stand a lot of racket. Couldn't he just go and live somewhere else?"

"Well, my friend, that's the problem. Nobody else has been willing to give him a chance and he's going crazy here. He can't stand being in a cage. I think he'll calm down once he has a home. He's young, and I can see from this meeting that he knows you're the boss. He won't be any threat to you. Won't you please give him a chance? You have a great opportunity here to share your home and to teach him all about what it feels like to be loved."

"Yeah, yeah. Okay, since you put it that way. Tell him it's fine."

"No, Swede. You tell him. He needs to hear from you that he's welcome. I know that your humans like him, but you're the one he'll be depending on to teach him, and he needs to know that you approve. Let's join your people and Andrew to give you a chance to tell him you're okay about him living with you."

We caught up to the others and I walked Swede next to Andrew so they could talk. I couldn't hear what was being said, but after a few minutes Andrew turned to me with a big grin pasted on his face and I knew that Swede had given his blessing.

My friends thought Andrew was wonderful and were excited about welcoming him into their home. They headed to the office to take care of paperwork while I walked both dogs to the parking lot. When my friends returned I said that I'd drive Andrew to their house in my truck, which would give me a chance to say goodbye to him and see him settled in his new home.

I also thought it would be wise for me to drive Andrew to his new home because I didn't want to push the already fragile relationship between Swede and Andrew by putting them too close together in my friends' car. I knew that the dogs would be fine in time, but it was too soon to ask Swede to be up close and personal with Andrew in a small moving vehicle. Even though I knew Andrew would try to be careful, he was liable to bounce around and Swede could become irritated with him before they even made it home. I wasn't willing to risk a possible disaster that would end with Andrew being brought back to the shelter.

Once he was in the truck with me, Andrew could hardly sit still. "They're really nice, Dale. Did you see? They brought me cookies and they didn't even know me. They said that they have a big yard, and on Sundays we'll get to go to the beach. Do you think they like me? Am I going to get to stay there forever? They won't bring me back will they? I couldn't stand that. Swede's okay. He's kinda old and I told him I'd take care of him. Oh Boy! I can hardly believe it. I'm gonna have a home and a family."

This non-stop monologue went on all the way to my friends' house and I could hardly get a word in edgewise, but I managed to reassure Andrew that everything would be fine. I told him that he wouldn't ever have to go back to the shelter because I knew that my friends were the kind of people who would somehow make this work. They understand how devastating it is for dogs to be adopted and then be brought back to the shelter because that's what had happened to Shad before they permanently adopted him.

After we arrived, I helped get Andrew situated and promised I'd come back to visit often, which I did … and still do.

Each time I visit Andrew, I'm so impressed by how he's adjusted to his new home, even though it did take him awhile to get used to the kindness and love that were offered to him by people outside of the shelter. Predictably, he didn't stop barking overnight, but the barking he does at home is different than the noise he made at the shelter. He loves announcing to the world that he's a happy dog. My friends have been incredibly patient with him, and he's quite calm now. He's always glad to see me, but it's clear that he knows he's home. Swede and he have worked things out between them and their relationship has become quite comfortable. Sometimes on Sundays I join them all at the beach, just to give life to my fantasy about seeing Andrew running on the beach. He's gained weight and his new name is Sport because my friends said that the name Andrew didn't fit him. I think the name Sport suits him well, and he seems to like it. He's content now … as shelter dogs will be if they're adopted by people who love them and are willing to create an opportunity for them to be happy members of a family.

The endless parade of dogs at the shelter waiting their turn to be adopted continues. Some days are long and lonely for them, but we all hope that there's someone out there for each of them. It's that hope that keeps a shelter volunteer going back day after day. Eventually many of the dogs find homes, but the waiting is so hard for them.

Want to hear my ultimate fantasy? My fantasy is actually a dream I have quite often. It goes like this:

I'm driving to the shelter, anxious to see all of the dogs and eager to hear about any adoptions that have happened since I was there last. When I drive into the parking lot, I don't hear any dogs barking. It's absolutely quiet. I sign in, grab a hand full of dog cookies and walk out to the cage area, ready to greet all of the dogs. I walk from cage to cage and see that every cage is empty. There isn't a single dog there! I run back to the office and there isn't anyone there either. I go back out to the cage area and once again walk past each cage. All empty. No dogs. Finally, I hear someone coming and turn to find the shelter manager standing there with a big smile on her face. She tells me that I don't need to walk dogs today because all of the dogs have been adopted.

All of the dogs have been adopted!

Now, that's a happy ending.

Don't I look great? Bet you never could tell that I'm the same dog you saw in the picture at the beginning of this story. Just goes to show what love and a great home will do for a dog.

I love being a Sport!

Regulars to the Rescue!

"Hey Duff, what's your hurry?"

"Oh, hi. Can't stop to talk now; I'm late for the meeting."

"Meeting? What meeting?"

"C'mon, walk with me and I'll tell you. There's this lost dog. All of us regulars are gonna get together to see if we can find her."

"Okay, maybe we can help. May we come to the meeting?"

"Sure, but give me some time to get there and then you and the other humans can join us later. We'll be over by the picnic area at Rocky Point. Gotta go, see ya later."

And with that, our friend Duff, the Scottie, raced away down the beach path to his meeting. I guess all of the beach walking regulars were at the gathering because there wasn't another dog around. I imagined a bunch of dogs having a conference and wondered who was in charge, but I figured that I'd find out soon enough when we joined them.

When we'd met Duff, my partner, Ellaine, and I were walking with our three Schnauzers, Joey, Pip and Fitz, but as soon as they heard what Duff had to say, they raced off with him. We weren't concerned because we knew where they were going, so we continued on our way, enjoying the mild winter day and being thankful, once again, that we live in such a beautiful place.

This island in the Pacific Northwest, this lovely bit of paradise, shows her beauty with many different faces: the oldest town in the state is nestled on the shores of a cove that welcomes whales and tall boats throughout the year; other small villages and artist communities appear along the highway that meanders through the center of the island; well tended farms protected by national reserve status stake their claims near the highway and in tucked away places discovered only by dirt or gravel roads; mussel flats can be seen in the waters near the center and south ends of the island; and nearly every weekend during the year the island hosts celebrations of harvest, art, fishing, music, and animals. This is a place where people with dogs are comfortable and welcome to enjoy the many beaches and trails available to them.

As we walked along we saw several boats not far from shore. Setting crab pots I assumed. By the time the crabbers were finished placing the pots, there would be hundreds of markers bobbing up and down. Off in the distance I could see the 10:45 ferry making its way to the mainland and the Victoria Clipper was moving along on its daily run. There's never a shortage of local color to be enjoyed on the water or on shore here.

This particular beach is a favorite when the tide is out because there's actually sand on which to walk instead of rocks. Also, tide pools are always a special treat when there's a low tide. School children often come on field trips to learn about life in the tide pools, but today the beach was deserted except for the seagulls, ravens, eagles, and our friend, York- a blue heron that stick-walked in the shallow water as he looked for breakfast.

"Hey, you two; have you seen Duff?"

We turned to see Duff's human companion coming up behind us, and we stopped so he could catch up.

"We saw him a few minutes ago. We were surprised that you weren't with him, but we figured you weren't far behind. He said he was on his way to a meeting over by the picnic area. Do you know what it's about? All he said was that there was a lost dog."

"No. Haven't got a clue. All I know is that we were walking along and all of a sudden Duff stopped and acted like he was listening real hard to something and then he took off running. I figured that I'd catch up with him eventually. Are your three with Duff?"

"Yeah, they all took off together. Walk with us and we'll see what the big meeting is all about."

The three of us walked together in that wonderful companionable silence that beach walkers understand. No need for conversation. We were just enjoying the day.

While we walked, I thought about Duff's relationship with his human. They'd been walking on this beach since Duff was a puppy, and Duff had his friend well trained. Duff loved to search for mice, and his human friend helped by turning over some of the bigger pieces of driftwood so Duff could find the mice. If his friend wandered too far away to help, Duff's imperious bark brought him back so he could do his job. It wasn't unusual for them to be out for several hours while Duff made sure that there were no critters running around. Duff was getting older, and he'd slowed down some, but his enthusiasm and sense of purpose never wavered.

As we came closer to the picnic area, we could see several other people arriving from various directions. It was funny to see them without their animal friends. When we walk on the beach every day, we get used to seeing the same human/animal combinations, and to see people without their dogs was disconcerting to say the least. It felt just as odd for us to be walking without our three in close attendance, but we knew where they were.

Finally, we walked over the sand dune that separates the picnic area from the beach, and there they were. It was like a scene out of a movie that could've been called *Dog Show At The Beach*. There were dogs of every imaginable breed and mix, all gathered in a circle, listening in various degrees of attentiveness to Sidney, a beautiful Standard Poodle that was pacing back and forth in front of them. Babette, Princess, Chablis, and Mon Petit Chou swarmed around his feet, doing their Miniature Poodle dance. I might have known that Sidney would be in charge; he has such presence.

"Okay, guys. Listen up. We've got a lost female dog somewhere around here and we need to find her. Duke, settle down and pay attention."

Duke, a young, enthusiastic black Lab mix, was chasing around the circle, trying to find someone to play with him, as he always did. "Okay, Sidney, okay. Don't nag; I'm cool."

"Excuse us, Sidney, but who's this lost dog?" "How do you know she's here?" These questions came from Georgie, a West Highland Terrier, and his companion, Baron, a Cairn Terrier, both stalwart little guys that were being attentive and polite.

"The lost dog is called Peaches and I know she's here because we saw her human looking for her and calling her yesterday."

"He's right." Blue, a handsome Collie/Shepherd mix with long legs was quick to respond. "I know because my human is the one looking for the dog. Peaches is a shelter dog that's visiting with us for a while, and she ran away yesterday when we were at the beach. I was the one that told Sidney about her and asked for this meeting."

"Well, maybe she doesn't want to be found. Maybe she's going home." This comment came from Rosy, a lively little Schnauzer who hopped around as she talked.

Blue gently disagreed with her. "If she really had a home, that might be true. But, remember, she's from the shelter. She's been there practically since she was born, and she wouldn't want to go back there, believe me. Besides, even though she's only about a year old, she's shy and kinda scared. She's a big Rottweiler, but she doesn't know how big she is."

"We're wasting time here." Cody, a Husky/Shepherd mix, was a canine of action. He was ready to search. "Let's go and find her."

"But, what about our people?" Shad, a chocolate Poodle, was worried. He never strayed far from his human, and going off on a search without his friend clearly bothered him.

Daisy, an American Eskimo, and Shad's adopted sister, reassured him by nose pointing over in our direction. By now, all human companions of the dogs at the meeting were gathered round, listening to the conversation. "Look over there, Shad. Our people are here too. They'll help."

"How can I help? I can't even see." Swede, a sweet old Lab that was blind, quietly asked his question.

"You can stay here and wait while we look." Swede's younger brother, Sport, a Lab/Husky mix, reassured him. "You'll know she's here if she comes around. If she does, you can watch over her 'til we get back."

"I wanna stay with Swede. I'm too small to go running around. I might get lost too, and then you guys'd be looking for two of us." Harry, a tiny Chihuahua, jumped up on a table so everyone could see and hear him.

"Maybe I'd better stay with Swede and Harry." This was our Fitz. "I can't see very well either and my hearing's not so good."

Joey and Pip, our other two canine friends that were sitting next to Fitz, leaned into him and Joey said, "Good idea, Fitz. Pip and I will go with everybody else." Joey, as always, was raring to go, and I could see that he was jazzed being around all of his buddies.

By now, the dogs were getting restless and seemed ready to go off in every direction until Baron spoke up. "Calm down everybody. Let Sidney talk."

Just the mention of Sidney's name settled everyone. He took advantage of the moment to give directions.

"Thanks, Baron. Okay gang, here's the plan. Duff, you take Georgie and Baron and look over in the woods behind us. Blue, you take Duke and Sport with you and head on over to the golf course. You guys can run fast and cover lots of ground. Duke, you be sure and stay with them and don't go off chasing golf balls. Keep your mind on your job. Joey, you and Pip know the beach to the left really well, so you take Rosy and Cody with you and search the beach area toward Henry's Beach. Don't forget the area up on top near the trees. I'll take my little guys with me, and we'll head the other direction down the beach. Harry, you stay here with Swede and Fitz."

"But what about me, Sidney? And Shad? We can search in the marsh area." How predictable that Daisy would want to search in the marsh. Every time we saw her, the little rascal's beautiful white coat was wet and slimy because she'd found something interesting in the mucky water.

"Okay, Daisy, fine. You and Shad can look around the marsh."

Pip was worried. "But, Sidney, if this dog is lost, how come we can't tune in to her like we always do if someone needs help? Why can't we sense where she is? Why can't we hear her heart-talk to us?"

Sidney was quick to respond and what he said made good sense. His answer concerned me too. "The fact that we can't pick up on her might mean that she's badly hurt and isn't able to send out any kind of distress signal. That's why we have to hurry. Every once in a while I get a faint message, but I can't tell where it's coming from."

By now all of us humans who'd been listening had moved closer to the dog circle, and I was the first to speak. "Sidney, how can we help? Shouldn't we go with our guys to be sure everyone is safe?"

"Well, of course, Dale. I assumed that you'd all be going with your friends. The more of us out there, the quicker we'll find Peaches. Let's give ourselves about two hours and we'll meet back here. You humans can keep track of your own time. C'mon everybody, let's find Peaches."

No further encouragement needed, all of the dogs and humans sorted themselves out and went off in their assigned directions. Ellaine stayed with Fitz, and I went off with Joey, Pip and the rest of our little group.

The beach was piled with huge pieces of driftwood because of the high tides that had slammed into shore recently, so we had to do more than just look on the beach. We really had to poke around in the driftwood too. Well, I say, "we," but the dogs did the poking. They were so thorough that they examined behind, around and under every pile of driftwood between the picnic area at Rocky Point and the barbecue pits at Henry's Beach. It took us almost an hour to go a fairly short distance, but by the time we arrived at our destination, we felt pretty sure that we hadn't missed anything.

Joey, Pip, Cody and Rosy raced up the hill while the three of us human companions walked up behind them. Rosy's short little legs churned furiously, but she had no trouble keeping up with the other dogs. Before we even got to the top, the dogs were looking around the bushes in the treed area. They'd split up so they could cover more territory, and we trailed along behind them. I don't think they needed us, but we helped them search anyway.

After about forty-five minutes, I called to the dogs and told them we'd best get back to Rocky Point. On the way back, we all took the inside trail. We'd covered the beach and driftwood on the way up, but we'd saved the trail for the return trip. We didn't want to miss anything; unfortunately, there wasn't anything to miss. We all listened as hard as we could, but no one heard anything. Peaches was nowhere to be found.

By the time we got to the picnic area, almost everyone was reassembled. Dogs and humans were tired, but nobody was smiling. We gathered up the water jugs that all of us keep in our vehicles and set water out for the thirsty dogs. While they drank their fill, we all made our reports to Sidney. The news was short and discouraging.

No one had seen Peaches. No one had heard Peaches. No one knew where she was.

But, no one wanted to give up.

"Okay, everybody, here's what we do." Sidney in charge again. "Does anybody have any food with them?"

Several people said that they did and immediately went to their cars to get what they had.

"We need to leave food in several different places so that in case Peaches comes around here, she'll at least have something to eat."

If she can still eat, I thought to myself. But, as quickly as the thought had flown into my head, I dismissed it and welcomed a more positive picture.

"That's right, Dale. You've got the idea." Sidney was pacing again. "We all need to see Peaches well and safe. We can't find her with negative energy. We need to focus on her as a healthy and happy dog. She'll respond to a positive picture."

"But, what do we do now?" "We can't leave; somebody has to stay." Swede and Fitz, the senior members of the group, were reluctant to go home, even though they each could probably have used a good long nap.

Blue's human friend, Anne, walked to the center of the group. "Everybody's tired, and we know she isn't around here right now. I suggest that we put food out, make some signs and post them everywhere in this area, go door to door at the houses nearby, and meet here again tomorrow to do another search together. If any of you want to come back later today or tonight, that would be wonderful."

Everyone agreed that these were good ideas, so after putting out food, deciding who was going to make signs and agreeing on who would take which house, we all went our separate ways for the day, knowing that some of us would be back later.

This process went on for three days. Each day we returned we saw that some of the food had been eaten, but with so many raccoons, rabbits, ravens, gulls and eagles in the area, we had no way of knowing which animal or bird was eating the food. Still we continued to search.

Finally, on the fourth day we found her. Or rather, she found us. We'd all dispersed to search our assigned areas and were back at the picnic area waiting for the golf course guys to join us. They were late. We hoped it was for good reason. As we sat around waiting, we kept looking toward the golf course, eagerly hoping to see Blue, Sport and Duke come running with Peaches trotting happily alongside of them.

That wasn't exactly what we saw. In the distance, what looked like some kind of bizarre funeral procession, made its way toward us, except that the "casket" was a blue tarp. A large dog, that surely must be Peaches, lay motionless on the tarp, while Blue, Sport, Duke and their humans dragged her toward us.

Those of us waiting all rushed toward the little procession that moved ever so slowly in our direction. When we reached them and there were enough humans to carry the unconscious dog, we all moved to the grass area and gently laid her down.

The dogs were calm, but the humans were all talking at once.

"Is this Peaches?"

"Is she dead?"

"Where did you find her?"

The questions all blurred together until finally Anne interrupted with some information.

"Yes, this is Peaches, and no, she's not dead. I think her leg is broken and she's unconscious because she's dehydrated and she probably has a concussion. There's a big lump on her head. She's pretty banged up, and we need to get her to a vet right away. She's so heavy that even the three of us couldn't carry her all the way back here, but we found a ratty old tarp in the bushes and we managed to lay her on it and drag her back here. Strong hands and even stronger teeth did the trick."

Duff's human had a van and was busy spreading blankets in the back so that Peaches could be transported as soon as possible. While we, the humans, were lifting Peaches into the van, all of the dogs moved as close to her as possible, whispering, licking, offering reassurance and comfort. Harry was so anxious to do something that he jumped up on Peaches and energetically licked her face, just willing her to wake up. He hardly weighed anything, so nobody stopped him. There was so much loving energy whirling around that the air was positively electrified.

And then she opened her eyes. Peaches looked at all of us crowded around the sliding door of the van and she smiled. Yes!

"Wow. You guys heard me. I knew you would. I knew it."

Her voice was faint, but she was conscious.

We made her comfortable and I turned to Anne. "How did you find her? Where was she?"

"She found us. We were up in a treed area behind the back of the golf course and we heard her calling. Well, actually, Blue, Sport and Duke heard her. They went racing off to a grove of trees that we obviously hadn't searched very well before, and there she was, lying in some bushes. After we determined that she was still breathing, we had to figure out how to get her back. The three of us humans tried to carry her, but she's so heavy we couldn't manage and we were afraid that we'd hurt her if we continued. We used that old tarp we found as a stretcher, and here we are. Now, we need to get her to a vet right away."

Blue and Anne rode in the back of the van with Peaches, while Duff and his human drove them to the nearest vet. I drove Anne's car so she would have a way home from the vet, and Ellaine took our car with Joey, Pip and Fitz. Everyone else followed in his or her own vehicle. None of us were going home until we knew that Peaches would be all right.

Our parade of vehicles roared into town and we all parked somewhat haphazardly at our local veterinary clinic. I jumped out and went in first to make sure that Ken was ready to receive our precious patient. Fortunately he wasn't with a client at the moment, and he quickly went outside and supervised the bringing in of Peaches. Because we knew he didn't want or need a crowd inside, while Anne and Blue went in with Peaches, the rest of us waited in our vehicles.

After what seemed like a long time, Blue and Anne came out with big smiles on their faces. As soon as we saw them, all of us- dogs and humans- jumped out of our respective vehicles and gathered around for the news. Two people were walking around in the garden shop next door, and they stared at us in amazement. I can only imagine what they must have thought, but we didn't care about them right then.

"She's going to be all right." Anne was speaking now. "She did break her leg, but Ken thinks it will heal fine because she's so young. He's giving her fluids now because she's so dehydrated, and he's going to take x-rays, but he thinks she'll make a full recovery."

Human cheering and dog barking were boisterous echoes of our feelings. Wonderful news.

"She'll get to come home with you, won't she? She won't have to stay here, will she?" Shad anxiously looked at Anne for reassurance.

"She'll need to stay for a couple of hours, but Blue and I will stay with her. Then, when she's ready, we can take her home."

"But, how 'ya gonna get her home? She's really big!"

"Don't worry, Harry. I'm going to call my husband and he'll come with our van. Ken has a stretcher large enough for Peaches; the office assistants and the three of us will be able to carry her to the van. After we get home, our neighbors will help us carry her into the house. It'll be fine."

"I know it's probably none of my business, but will she have to go back to the shelter?" Sidney was pacing again. "Doesn't seem fair, after all she's been through, that she has to go back there."

"I called the shelter while we were inside, and they said I could keep her at my house until she's recovered. After she's well, we'll make a serious effort to find her a home."

"She can come and live with us, can't she?" Duke was standing with his front legs on the shoulders of his human as he talked. "We have lots of room, don't we? You've been looking for a friend for me and I want Peaches. She's big, like me, and we could have lots of fun. Please. Please."

"We'll see, Duke. We can go and visit her while she's at Blue's house and after she's well, we'll see."

I smiled to myself. A done deed … how perfect.

Our dog and human rescue organization finally left Ken's office. We didn't have to say anything about seeing each other again, because we knew that we'd all be doing our beach walks and the regulars would be meeting and greeting as always.

That was two months ago. During the time she was at Blue's house, all of us took turns going to visit Peaches, and each time we saw her, she looked better and better. And, during our various visits we got her to tell us what had happened to her.

"Well, gee, I didn't mean to get lost. I'd never been able to run free before and I guess I went a little crazy. When Anne dropped my leash by accident, I took off. All I could think was that I was free. I ran and ran as fast as I could. It felt so good to stretch my legs that I didn't pay any attention to where I was or what I was doing. I wasn't running away from her; I was just running. After a while, I didn't know where I was and I got kinda scared. Nothing looked familiar, but then I'd never been to the beach before, so I didn't know how to get back there from wherever I was. I was in a bunch of trees and got tangled up in some bushes. When I tried to get out, my leg got twisted and I felt it break. That freaked me out and when I tried to get up, I hit my head on a tree. I guess I got knocked out because when I woke up it was dark."

"I couldn't move because I was caught in a bunch of old wire that was lying around. I was stuck. The more I tried to get free, the more stuck I got. Finally I stayed where I was. My head hurt and I kept passing out. I guess I was there for days, but I didn't know it. I knew that I was cold, hungry, thirsty and dizzy. I didn't see or hear anybody, so I figured I was in some place where nobody ever came. I tried to bark, hoping somebody might hear me, but I knew that nothing much was coming out. I sent help messages too, but I was weak and I didn't think that anyone could hear me. Finally I heard Blue. I guess I smelled him and the other guys, Duke and Sport. I concentrated as hard as I could and pretty soon I could feel that they heard me. You know the rest. I'm happy you guys found me. I don't think I could've lasted much longer."

Not only did Peaches make a full recovery, but today at the beach we saw a sight that transformed the whole rescue experience into a marvelous happy ending.

When we arrived at the beach parking lot, we saw the car belonging to Duke's human and so we knew he couldn't be far away. I grabbed my old sweatshirt from the backseat because Duke was a very enthusiastic greeter and he was usually wet and smelly. Joey, Pip and Fitz raced to the beach while we trudged after them. We looked both directions and in the distance to the left we saw two happy dogs playing in the surf.

Our friend Joey, the official beach greeter, took off in their direction and soon all three dogs were running toward us. Well, two of them were running and the third was limping to keep up.

Duke had a friend. Not just any friend, but a special friend. He and Peaches came skidding up to us and almost knocked us over in their enthusiasm. Joey was so excited he could hardly talk.

"Look who's here! It's Peaches! She lives with Duke now! Isn't that great? She can even run … sort of."

Both big dogs flopped down on the beach and Duke placed a paw protectively on the back of his new friend as if to say, 'Mine. This is my sister.' He grinned and Peaches wore a smile that was so wide we thought her jaws would come apart.

It wasn't any surprise to us that Peaches had been adopted by Duke's family, but it was wonderful to actually see them together and to know it was true. There were lots of hugs, kisses and more love than I could describe in our meeting this morning. Duke has his very own sister. Peaches has a family who loves her.

But the best part is that we share their world … and they share ours.

We all create our own reality and I really like this one. It's a beautiful day.

Just beautiful.

Sushi the Wonder Dog

My friend Nancy was addressing a group of parents who had come to hear her talk about a new program she was initiating at the high school. She was a tall, imposing woman, dressed for the occasion in what she called her "power outfit" - bright yellow blazer, white silk blouse, and black slacks. Her favorite tennis shoes had even been replaced with low black heels. She was every bit the well dressed, professional educator. Except that she held a scrawny, unkempt, almost white dog in her arms.

Nancy's presentation was animated, as always. As she walked and talked in front of the group of people who had come to meet the woman who would be teaching their kids, she shifted the dog from arm to arm, never missing a beat. She talked for about thirty minutes, but she never mentioned the dog. I watched her audience and they were hooked. But then, Nancy had a way of doing that with people. She was charming, enthusiastic, and completely at ease in front of any crowd. I knew that the folks who had come to hear her were thinking that they'd love to have their kids in her class any day. Others were probably thinking that they'd love to be in her class. She completed her presentation, answered questions, and then sat down. No one asked her about the dog.

I took over my part of the meeting, introducing others involved in the program, and then opened a discussion for general questions. Finally, one lady couldn't resist.

"I can't help but be curious. Mrs. Matlock, why do you have your dog here tonight?"

Nancy laughed and stood up, the dog still plastered to her chest. "This is my friend, Sushi. She wasn't feeling well today, so I brought her with me. I think she ate something that disagreed with her and she's probably fine, but no one's home and I didn't want her to be sick at home by herself."

At the time, I don't think Nancy had any idea how soon Sushi would be returning the favor.

Sushi the puppy had become a part of Nancy's life many years before when Nancy found her at the local animal shelter and couldn't resist taking her home because, as Nancy said, "She was the funniest looking dog I'd ever seen. She looked like the Heartworm Poster Dog. I didn't think anyone would ever adopt her, so I said that we had to have her. It was love at first sight."

And so it was. This scrawny, hair-sticking-out-in-every-direction little dog took one look at her new friend and claimed her. When she was first adopted, Sushi fit in the palm of Nancy's hand, and only grew to weigh a puny eleven pounds. But she was all heart. And, she knew that she had a job to do.

Not long after the parent meeting, Nancy was diagnosed with ovarian cancer. Initially, she agreed to have the necessary chemotherapy and radiation treatments, and for a time the cancer seemed to have disappeared. Then one day she called and said that she'd been in for some tests and all indications were that the cancer had reappeared with a vengeance. She said that she'd discussed the situation with her family and with their reluctant blessing, she'd decided that she'd had enough. She had battled several life threatening illnesses over a twenty-year period and she was tired. She knew that she was dying; yet she wanted to continue to teach as long as she could, and then stay at home with her family until the time came for her to leave them.

And that's what she did. The cancer progressed rapidly, and soon Nancy gave up teaching (at least in the traditional sense) and was unable to leave her home. At first she was able to get around the house, but eventually she couldn't leave her bed. Hospice provided assistance, and Nancy's husband, mother, daughter, son and wife were there doing what they could to make her comfortable.

Then there was Sushi.

Sushi greeted everyone who came to see Nancy and ushered them into her room. She even monitored the length of the visits, and when someone was staying too long, and she knew that her friend was tiring, she became restless. Nancy would take her cue from Sushi, and tell her visitor that it was time to leave. On one particular day when I came to visit, Sushi came to meet me as she always did, and I had an opportunity to talk with her.

"Hey, Sush, how's it going? Are you holding up okay?"

"Hi, Dale, it's going fine, I guess. Everybody here is pretty sad and scared, but I'm doing okay. I'm just staying close to my friend. She's hanging on pretty tight these days, but that's why I'm here."

"I know, little one, I know. I'm so glad you're here for her. She really needs you."

Nancy recognized her need too and was able to verbalize what Sushi meant to her on that same day. I was sitting next to the bed and Sushi was in her usual position on the bed, resting her head on Nancy's stomach.

"You know, Dale, this little sweetheart is an amazing source of comfort for such a small dog. I can't get over how much energy I can draw from her. Like right now, with her head resting on my stomach, I can feel some of the pain going away."

"Yeah, I can see that. So tell me, what is it that Sushi gives you that you can't get from the rest of your family?"

'That's easy. No fear. No guilt. No regrets. No sadness. No anger. Just pure love. My family loves me, of course, but they're so consumed by sadness that it's hard for them to be with me sometimes. They're already grieving for me and I'm not even dead yet. Sushi lives in the moment. She's teaching me how to do that. It's not an easy lesson, but I think I'm getting the hang of it."

With Sushi's help, Nancy was not only teaching herself how to live in the moment, but she was teaching the rest of her family as well. If Sushi knew that it was time for someone to take a break, she ran to get her leash and demanded that she be taken out for a walk. When the family needed a distraction, Sushi entertained them with her silly antics. She had a great sense of humor, maybe because she figured any dog that looked as ridiculous as she did, had to be able to laugh and make people laugh. More often than not, when I came to visit I found Nancy and her family laughing and talking together, or even reading to each other. Sometimes, just holding on and crying. But, definitely being in the moment.

One day, after Nancy had moved to a hospital bed that had been installed in the bedroom, I arrived and saw Nancy's husband reading to her. Sushi was under the bed blissfully playing with all of her squeaky toys, making contented noises that could be heard over the sound of reading. Every once in a while Nancy's husband would stop reading and he and Nancy would laugh at the noise Sushi was making with her toys. Sushi was participating in the experience in the only way she knew how.

The hospital bed was too high for Sushi to jump on by herself, so she stationed herself next to the bed until someone came along to help her up. She knew that Nancy was in a great deal of pain, even with the morphine drip, so she carefully positioned herself on the bed. She was always touching some part of Nancy's body without creating any painful pressure.

Finally the time came for Nancy to make her departure. She had lapsed into a coma, and we all knew it wouldn't be long before she physically left us. Sushi knew that her friend was almost Home, and so she began to divert her attention to the rest of the family. She followed everyone around, and at first Nancy's family didn't quite get what she was doing.

"Dale, what's up with Sushi? Why is she following me around? Why isn't she in with Mom?" Nancy's daughter was almost exasperated in her effort to understand Sushi's actions.

"She knows that your mom doesn't need her anymore, but you do. She's offering you what comfort and attention she can give. Let her take care of you."

Later that night, Nancy finally stopped breathing and made her journey Home. As we sat in the living room drinking coffee after the body had been removed, Sushi made the rounds, sitting on laps and being wonderfully attentive to all of us. After she'd touched base with each person, she crawled up on the couch and just watched everyone. Ever vigilant. She was calm and her presence seemed to soothe everyone in the room

Before she died, Nancy had asked me to conduct her memorial service, and a couple of days before the service, I talked to Sushi about what I wanted to do.

"Sush, I'd like you to be with me. I'd like to be holding you while I talk to people about your friend. Are you willing to come along?"

"Oh, Dale, that isn't necessary. You know how I hate crowds. I don't need to be there. I know that my friend will be there because she wouldn't miss her own celebration, but she and I dream together all the time now and I don't need to come. You go and do your thing. I'll just hang out at home."

"Are you sure? Seems like you should be there along with the rest of the family."

"No, really, but I'll be there in spirit, as you'd say."

I saw that she was firm about not going, and so I didn't press the issue any further. We did the memorial service and at one point I talked about how much Sushi had helped Nancy and her family. Those who knew Sushi smiled as I talked about her, and I think some wished that she'd been with us at the celebration too. She was there, though. I felt her presence, just as I felt the presence of the woman she loved. The barriers we create surrounding death aren't real. They don't exist. Not at all.

After Nancy's death, the Matlock family tried as best they could to resume their lives, but it wasn't easy. Nancy was a strong presence while she was with them, and coping with her physical absence was difficult for them. Sushi helped as much as she could, but she found herself spending a great deal of time home alone because the rest of the family needed to keep busy as part of their grieving process. It was hard for them to be in that house so filled with memories of Nancy.

One day I stopped by the Matlock house and found Sushi there by herself. In fact, she was out on the front lawn, looking down the street toward the woods.

"Sushi, what are you doing out here? How did you get out?"

"Oh, hi Dale. I know how to get the back door open. Nobody's home, so I'm out here sitting in the sun."

"Are you all right? Do you want me to talk to the family about spending more time at home so you aren't alone so much?"

"No. No. Don't be silly. They're doing what they have to do. I'm fine. My job is finished here, and I'm hanging out for a while until it's time for me to move on. Everything is as it should be. Don't worry."

"Well, if you say so. How about a walk?"

"Sure, let's walk into the woods. I've been going there a lot lately. There're some great smells there and it's quiet and peaceful. I like it."

When Sushi said she'd been going to the woods, I assumed that someone had been taking her for walks there. But I was wrong; she'd been taking herself for walks there.

I never discussed this conversation with the family. Sometimes I wonder if I should have, but I know that telling them wouldn't have changed anything. Sushi knew what she was doing.

Several weeks later, I got a frantic phone call from Nancy's daughter. "We can't find Sushi anywhere! She isn't in the house. We've looked all over and she's just gone!"

"Calm down, Jen. Has this happened before?"

"Yeah, a couple of times lately we came home and she was gone. We always found her nearby in the woods, but we had no idea how she got there."

"Have you looked in the woods today?"

"That's the first place we looked. We've been out there for hours and she isn't there. We don't know where else to look. I don't understand what's going on. Where is she?"

"You know where she is, Jen. Think about it."

"That's all we've been doing. After it got dark and we couldn't see to search anymore- even with flashlights- we came back home. We've been sitting here doing nothing but thinking and talking about her."

"So, what have you come up with?"

"Well, this sounds crazy, but we think she's gone to be with Mom. I think she figured that we didn't need her anymore and she just …went away."

"That sounds right to me. Are you okay with her being gone?"

"Yes. No. I don't know. I feel so guilty. She's been by herself so much lately because we've all been gone. I feel like we've neglected her and now she isn't here anymore. What do you think?"

"I think that she went to be with your mom. Also, I think that her wandering off lately has been her way of telling you that she needs to be somewhere else. Kind of like rehearsing the real thing. Don't beat yourself up about neglecting her. She knows that you've all been doing what you need to do. I don't know where her body is, but I know that she's gone Home. Let her go."

The conversation went on a few minutes longer, but finally Jennifer said that she thought she understood. I knew that she'd continue to look the next day, but I also knew that she wouldn't find Sushi. That night I dreamed about Sushi and she was exactly where I knew she'd be.

Sushi and Nancy were walking in a field of wildflowers. Well, Nancy was walking. Sushi was in her arms, plastered to her chest, looking up at her friend with a huge smile. Nancy shifted Sushi in her arms, turned, waved, and they were gone.

Sushi the Wonder Dog was Home.

Well done, my friend. Well done.

The B.G.s

It was the smell that got to me first. Obviously they hadn't heard of aroma therapy here. Or, if they had, I couldn't imagine what kind of therapeutic results they expected when the "aroma" was a combination of disinfectant, sickly sweet perfume, urine, stale cooking smells and lord knows what else. It was a terrible odor and I hadn't even gone beyond the front door.

Breathing through my mouth, I managed to get past the door and found myself in kind of a common room. What I saw, combined with the smell, was enough to give me second thoughts about taking another step, but I was here for a purpose, and so I kept walking. A large television was blaring in the corner. Old people sat around like wilting flowers mindlessly watching "Wheel of Fortune." Empty eyes. No one spoke. No one even looked up when I came farther into the room.

There was a reception desk toward the back of the room and so I headed in that direction, walking past the people who seemed pasted to their chairs. Maybe that was it. Maybe this was just an illusion, and if I went out the door and came back in again, I'd see something different. I hesitated long enough to consider the thought when I heard a voice. Aha! Someone was breathing after all.

"May I help you?" The woman sitting behind the reception desk had noticed me and was trying to get my attention. Too late to leave now.

"Yes, you can. I'm here to see Louisa."

"Oh, go on down the hall, take a left, and keep going until you get to room 21." With that, she turned back to the computer screen on her desk (which I noticed was showing a solitaire game). Very busy day.

Since there didn't seem to be any more conversation happening here, I went down the hall, took a left, and looked for room 21. As I walked, I felt as though I were running some kind of wheelchair gauntlet. In front of each door along the hallway sat a person in a wheelchair. Some were sleeping. Some were just staring off into space. One woman kept picking at the sleeve of her sweater. Another woman was muttering something I couldn't quite hear and when I walked past her she grabbed the sleeve of my jacket.

"Help me. Please help me. Help me. Please help me." She kept repeating the same phrases over and over again.

I bent down and took her hand in mine. "What can I do to help you?"

She continued to hang on to my jacket and repeated the same words again. I didn't feel like she was really seeing me, but she must have known I was there because she still held my arm. I repeated myself too. "What can I do to help you?"

Then she begged for help again. I realized that there wasn't any point in continuing this repetitive exchange, so I gently disengaged my arm and went back down the hall to the reception desk. I hated to interrupt the solitaire game, but I naively thought the woman at the desk might be able to help the lost soul in the hallway.

"Oh, that's Annie. She says that all the time. Just ignore her." That was the response I got.

"But, isn't there something that someone can do for her? She's obviously distressed."

"Nope, that's just the way she is." She went back to her game of solitaire.

No help there. I went back down the hallway and stopped again in front of Annie. And once again, she grabbed my arm.

"Annie, I'd like to help you. What do you need?"

She looked at me with vacant eyes and kept repeating the same phrases over and over. I stayed for a few minutes, holding her hand, and the physical contact did seem to quiet her and she actually stopped talking for a few seconds. Finally, I patted her hand and told her I'd be back. She didn't acknowledge me in any way, but I think she may have heard me.

I continued on down the hall until I reached room 21. The door was closed, so I knocked quietly before entering the room. There were two beds in the room. The bed closest to the door was empty, but there was someone in the other bed near the glass sliding doors that led out to a small patio. It appeared that the woman was sleeping, so I walked quietly over to her bed and sat down in a chair that was near the foot of the bed. She wasn't sleeping. She was lying on her side, staring out at the patio. She probably hadn't heard me come in because she didn't appear to know I was there. Maybe I was invisible. Neither the receptionist nor Annie had really known I was there either. It was time for a reality check.

"Excuse me, are you Louisa?"

At the sound of my voice, the woman turned toward me and carefully scooted herself up in the bed so she could look at me. "Yes, I am. What do you want?"

"My name's Dale. I came to visit with you for a while."

"Why? I don't get visitors. I don't even know you." She had a very commanding voice, and I immediately felt like I was back in third grade.

In my very best adult voice, desperately trying to overcome the third grade child in me, I told her why I was there. "I'm here because an old friend of yours told me that you like dogs."

Well, I guess I'd said the magic word. When I mentioned "dogs" she sat up straighter, her eyes softened and there was even a hint of a smile waiting to emerge. It wasn't there yet, but I could see the potential.

"What friend? I don't have any friends anymore. They're all dead like I will be soon."

"Your friend Bud told me about you. He's very much alive, and he's concerned about you."

"How do you know Bud? And, if he's so concerned, why doesn't he come by and see me?"

"Bud and I have a mutual friend and that's how we met. He doesn't come to see you because he's been in the hospital recovering from surgery. He says he'll visit you as soon as he's able." I continued by telling her more about how I'd met Bud, our mutual friend, and on and on.

All of this talk about Bud and how I knew him didn't interest her. I could tell. The light that I'd briefly seen in her eyes was fading, and I knew that if I didn't get the conversation back on track I'd lose my audience.

"So, is it true?" I took a break from my Bud monologue to interject this question.

"Is what true?" She was back to staring outside again.

"That you like dogs. I understand from Bud that you've welcomed many dogs into your home."

"Yes, it's true. My home and my heart." Her voice was softer now. Not quite so strident and impatient. "I miss them so much." Now I could see tears beginning to form at the corners of her eyes.

Louisa's friend Bud had told me that when Louisa had fallen and broken her hip, she had spent several weeks in the hospital, and then her family had moved her from the hospital to Rainbow Retreat. She was eighty-two and she needed physical therapy as well as skilled nursing care. Her dogs were taken to the shelter where they were euthanized because no homes could be found for them, and they weren't welcome at Rainbow Retreat. Two beautiful elderly Labrador Retrievers died because no one wanted them. And their friend was here in this depressing place, dying by inches herself.

"I know you must miss them. That's why I'm here."

Louisa tried to sit up even straighter as she listened to me. "What do you have to do with my dogs? Are you bringing them to see me? Are you taking me to see them?" She was anxious now, and quite animated. "I've been so worried about them, and no one will tell me how they are. No one tells me anything."

Oh, no. She didn't know they were dead. Why hadn't her family told her? Was it up to me to break the news to her? I didn't even know her. Would I be trespassing on someone else's territory if I did? Well, I knew that I couldn't lie to her. She deserved to be treated with respect and to know the truth, no matter how difficult it might be to hear.

While these thoughts were churning around in my head, I looked back at her and I could see in her eyes that she realized they were gone.

She did. "They're dead aren't they? I can see by the look on your face that they are. No one told me." She slumped back down in the bed and turned toward the sliding doors, tears streaming down her face.

I moved my chair closer to the head of the bed and took her hand. "Listen, Louisa. I shouldn't be the one to tell you this, but I won't lie to you. Yes, they're gone. The shelter couldn't find homes for them, and they were euthanized. I'm so sorry. I thought you knew."

"Please leave me alone. I still don't know you, and I don't care why you came. I don't want to talk anymore." She pulled her hand from mine, and turned away from me even more.

"I will go, but not before I tell you why I came. I'm here because I have two dog friends that I'd like you to meet. I thought that you knew your dogs were gone, and I felt you might like some dog company. I know you can't have animals live with you here, but if you'd like, I'll check with the management and see if I may bring my friends to visit you. I'm sure they won't mind." (I wasn't sure at all, but I was going to do my best to make it happen if Louisa wanted to meet my friends.)

She was listening, but she was still turned away from me. "Why would you do that? What's the point?"

"The point is that you're here and you're obviously depressed. You don't get to touch any dogs here. You don't get to hug them or smile with them. That can't be easy for someone who loves animals. I know it would be impossible for me."

"They probably won't let you bring dogs here. Why bother?"

"I'll tell you what. Why don't I go and find out? If they say yes, would you be willing to meet my friends?"

She didn't respond and I took her silence to mean that she might be willing, so I left the room before she could say anything else and went back down the hall to the reception desk. The wheelchair people weren't in front of their doors any longer; I assumed that they'd been taken back into their rooms. When I returned to the desk, the solitaire game was still in progress. The woman looked up at me, "DON'T BOTHER ME" written in big letters all over her forehead.

"Now what?" Obviously this lady was a Miss Manners Charm School dropout.

"I won't take much of your time because I know you're busy. Would it be permissible if I brought two older, very gentle dogs to see Louisa? They're always well behaved and won't bother anyone. She's very depressed and visiting with them might cheer her up."

"Sorry, no dogs allowed here."

Not so fast, lady. "Yes, I know that the patients can't have animals live here with them, but my two friends would be only visiting on occasion. Do you have any animal friends that live with you?"

Now she was actually looking at me. "Well, yes, I have two cats."

"Okay, think about how you'd feel if you couldn't see them or have them with you. Louisa's own dogs have been killed (no point in using the euphemism here when only straight talk would get this lady's attention), and she really misses them. Please, may I at least ask the person in charge if you don't have the authority to grant my request?"

While we were talking, a man walked out of an office behind the reception desk. He heard my question and asked if he could help me. I told him who I was, why I was there, and asked about having my friends come to visit Louisa.

"Well, I don't know. It's a bit irregular, but we have had animals come to visit on occasion. We haven't had any animals here recently, but I think somebody brought a cat to see a patient last year. I know Louisa and feel badly about her situation, but I can't have dogs running around here bothering the patients."

My foot was in the door and so I opened it wider. "Oh, they won't be running around at all. I'll keep them on leashes. They're very well behaved. I'll assume full responsibility for them. Why don't I bring them by tomorrow, and you can meet them before we go to visit Louisa?"

"Fine. Be sure you stop at the desk first."

I assured him that I would and made the trip back to Louisa's room. She was still lying on her side, looking away from me, but she turned toward me as I approached the bed.

"They said 'no', didn't they? I told you they would. Now, please go and leave me alone."

"Actually, Louisa, they said my friends could come tomorrow. If they pass inspection at the front desk, I can bring them back to see you. Is that okay with you?"

"I suppose. They'll probably change their minds, and I won't get to see them. Doesn't matter."

"It does matter, and I'll make sure that they pass whatever test Miss Solitaire and her boss have in mind. Don't worry. You'll get to meet them; I promise."

"Miss Solitaire? Who in the world is that?"

"She's the woman sitting behind the reception desk. Don't you ever get out into the common room where patients sit and watch television?"

"No, I haven't left my room since I got here last week. Just as well. I don't need to see a lot of old sick people. And I certainly don't want to watch television."

"If you don't ever leave your room, how do you spend your time? Aren't you doing any physical therapy for your hip?"

"I'm not interested in physical therapy. It's a waste of time since I won't ever be leaving here. I read, but mostly I stare out at the patio. Birds come to the tree out there and I watch them. At night when I can't see anything outside, I think about Rugby and Emma, my two dogs. And I sleep more and more each day. Passes the time."

"Well, tomorrow you'll have something interesting to see. You'll like my friends; I know you will. May I tell you about them?"

"I suppose. Even if I don't ever get to meet them, I love hearing about dogs."

"Their names are Alba and Malinche and they're English Labradors. Alba is almost thirteen, and she's a beautiful yellow, almost white color; Malinche is eleven and a half and is black. Alba is Malinche's mother and they've never been separated. I call them the B.G.s, short for 'big girls'. They're devoted to one another. Alba has arthritis and bad hips, but she gets around pretty well. Malinche loves the water and can chase a ball for hours. They don't live with me, but they visit often and I love them. They're wonderful girls. You'll see."

I watched Louisa's face as I talked about the dogs and each new bit of information brought a little more light into her eyes, and by the time I'd finished telling her about the girls, she was actually smiling. She was hooked and she hadn't even met the B.G.s yet.

I told her that she'd find out more tomorrow when she met them and then said that it was time for me to go, but I'd see her the next day.

After I arrived home I called Alba and Malinche's human friend, John, and told him about Louisa and my desire to have her meet the girls. He was happy to have them visit her and said he'd drop them off in the morning before he went to work.

The next morning the B.G.s came to visit. They've spent so much time at our house that they know the routine, and always head immediately for the drawer where we keep a supply of large dog cookies for them. After they'd had their cookies, they settled down and waited for the next event. John went off to work, and I asked the girls if they wanted to go for a ride and meet someone new.

"Sure, I'm up for a ride. Can we go to the beach?" "Who's the new friend? Does she play ball?" They both talked at the same time as they often did. Sometimes they even finished each other's thoughts. These two girls were really close. I sat down on the floor with them to tell them about Louisa. After I told them Louisa's story, they sat for a minute and then Alba, always a lady of few words, cut to the chase.

"Sounds like she needs us. Let's go."

As we drove to Rainbow Retreat, I told the girls that they'd have to pass inspection at the front desk before they met Louisa, and they both rolled their eyes but promised they'd be on their best behavior. They always were so I didn't doubt that they'd charm Miss Solitaire and her boss within seconds.

When we got out of the car, I attached both of their leashes and we went in and made our way to the front desk. While we were walking across the room, a few of the ever-present television watchers even looked at the dogs with interest. I wanted to take them around the room to meet everyone, but I didn't dare push my luck before they'd been given the green light by the person in charge. The others could meet them later. When we arrived at the front desk, Miss Solitaire actually noticed us and called over her shoulder to her boss, who must have been in his office. He came out and walked around the front of the desk to meet the girls.

To his credit, the man greeted the girls nicely and even petted them. They stood quietly and smiled at him while he ran his hands over their backs. "Good looking dogs. They don't bite, do they?"

"No, they don't bite. They're gentle and friendly. They're very social and are used to spending time with people." I went on to tell him how old they were, that they were mother and daughter, and anything else I could think of that would put his mind at ease.

After listening to me and watching the dogs, he said that they could visit Louisa, but we couldn't take the hallway to get to her room. He explained that he didn't want any of the other patients to see them in case somebody didn't like dogs, so he said we'd have to go out again and enter Louisa's room through the sliding doors near her bed.

He walked out with us and showed us which room was Louisa's and then said he'd go back in to Louisa's room and unlatch the sliding doors for us. This way of entering felt awkward and second class citizen-ish to me, but if that's what it took to get the girls inside, so be it.

"He's very uptight, isn't he?" Malinche had no trouble sizing him up. "Maybe I should have done my 'vicious dog' impersonation for him. That'd give him something to think about."

"Malinche, you're such a baby sometimes." Alba was being Mom. "Give the poor guy a break. He was okay."

We arrived at Louisa's room and, as we came closer, I could see her in the bed looking out through the sliding doors. When she saw the girls, she started to smile and cry at the same time. I opened the sliders, and the girls walked into the room and immediately went to the bed. Both of them rested their big beautiful heads on the bed next to Louisa's frail body, and Malinche, bless her heart, even put a paw up on the bed. Louisa reached out to both of them with her left hand while she tried to push herself up with her right arm.

I saw that she was having difficulty getting close enough to them, so I looked down at the foot of the bed for some kind of handle that would allow me to crank up the top portion of the bed. I found it and cranked until the bed was L-shaped. Now Louisa could sit with her back resting against the top part of the bed.

"That's better. Thank you. Oh, you girls are so beautiful. I didn't think I'd really get to see you. I can't believe you're here. Come closer. Please come closer."

As she talked, Louisa reached out with both arms and bent down far enough so that she could bury her face between the girls' heads. Alba and Malinche moved as close to her as they possibly could without climbing up on the bed. While I watched this wonderful meeting, I could see that the position was difficult for Louisa and asked her if there was a wheelchair in the room.

"Yes, there's one in the closet. You'll have to help me though. With my hip, I can't manage by myself."

I assured her that I would help and went to the closet to find the wheelchair. After I unfolded it and locked it into position, I wheeled it over to the bed. The girls knew what I was doing and moved aside so that I could get to Louisa. She was so thin and frail that I easily lifted her to the chair.

"Okay. Are you comfortable? Will this work?"

"Oh yes, that's better. Please put a pillow behind my back and one next to my left side because of my hip. I'll be fine."

Once I got her settled, the dogs immediately came back to her and got as close as they could. Now she could touch them with both hands without losing her balance.

"Alba. You must be Alba because you're white. You're the mother. And, Malinche. My, you're a big girl, aren't you? You're both big girls. Just like my Rugby and Emma. They were big too, only Rugby was a boy. You're so soft. It's been so long since I've touched a dog. You're both so beautiful."

She went on and on, chattering and being happy to spend time with the girls. The B.G.s were very attentive, too. They listened to every word she said and both gave her big slobbery kisses while she talked. Alba was more reserved than Malinche and she didn't always give kisses, but she knew that this lady really needed dog kisses so she happily obliged. At one point Louisa actually laughed out loud. That moment would have made a great photograph, but unfortunately I didn't have a camera. I'd remember to bring one next time so Louisa could have some pictures of her enjoying the dogs. She needed something to look at besides the small bare patio and a few birds in the tree. As I watched the love-in, I moved back to the corner of the room and quietly sat in a chair, wanting to give Louisa as much time alone with the girls as I could. I continued to eavesdrop, but I didn't want to be part of the conversation.

"Louisa, dear lady, how's your hip? I know about sore hips. Mine bother me too." Alba was talking softly, but giving Louisa her full attention.

"Oh, Alba, I guess it's healing, but it pains me most of the time. They say I should be able to use a walker soon, but I don't know if I have the strength to keep going. I feel so tired and sad all the time. I'd like to just slip away in my sleep some night. Then I could be with Rugby and Emma, and I wouldn't have to worry about this tired old body. I must say, though, that I feel wonderful right now. Having you and Malinche here makes me forget my pain."

"We're happy to see you too, Louisa. I'm sorry about your pain, but if having us here helps, then that's good."

Malinche put her paw on Louisa's arm to get her attention. "Did you ever play ball with your dogs? I love to play ball and I could teach you if you've never done it. It's fun, especially at the beach. Maybe we could all go to the beach some day. Or maybe, if there's a park near here, we could go there instead."

Louisa smiled, no doubt trying to imagine herself playing ball with this big lovable dog. "Well, of course, I used to play ball with Rugby all the time. Emma didn't much care for it, but Rugby loved chasing a ball. In fact, I found him in a dumpster when he was a puppy, and he had an old beat up football in his mouth; that's why I named him Rugby."

Malinche was persistent. "Good, so you know how to do it. You wouldn't have to throw it far. Or, Dale could throw the ball and you could watch."

"No, dear girl, if we're going to play ball some day, then I'm going to throw it for you. As soon as I'm able to get around a little better, we'll have an outing … maybe even a picnic. There's a park not far from here I'm told and we could go there. In the meantime, will you and Alba come to visit me often? I love having you here."

"Sure. We come to Dale's house all the time and she can bring us, just like today."

During the course of the next month there were many more "just-like-today"s for Louisa, Alba and Malinche. I brought the B.G.s to see her two or three times a week, and each visit proved to be more enjoyable than the last. Her hip was healing well, and she was able to spend more time in the wheelchair and less time in her bed. Sometimes, if the weather was nice, we went for a walk. I pushed the wheelchair and Alba and Malinche walked next to Louisa, one on each side of her. She never stopped touching them and they always made sure that they were in physical contact with her.

One day, about a month after our first visit, Louisa announced that she'd been doing the recommended physical therapy, and she was now able to use the walker that I saw in the corner of her room. She was eager to show us how she could manage and after shuffling around the room, she said that she wanted to go to the park to play ball with Malinche.

"I can't manage walking to the park yet, but I have permission from the office to have you drive us in your car. I can walk around once we're there."

No further encouragement needed, we all went outside through the sliding doors. Even though the B.G.s had been coming to visit for a month, they still had to use the outside entrance to go into Louisa's room - even on days when they visited with the patients in the common room before they went to see Louisa. Once we reached the car, Louisa managed to seat herself quite easily. I put her walker in the trunk, and we headed toward the park. Malinche was so excited she squirmed around like a little kid on her way to the ball game. She'd heard Louisa say that we were going to play ball and so the ball that she brought with her every time we came, but left in the car during the visit, was now firmly stuck in her mouth. It was a ratty old tennis ball, but she didn't care. It was a ball and that's all that mattered. She sat in the back seat with Alba, wearing a big goofy grin.

Once we got to the park, the dogs hopped out and patiently waited by the car while I helped Louisa out and brought her walker to her. There's a firm sand path that wanders through the park, and we set off on our walk. Malinche waited, oh, maybe three minutes, and then turned to Louisa and dropped the ball in front of her.

"Okay, Louisa, let's play ball!"

Bending down while still holding on to the walker was difficult for Louisa so I picked up the ball and handed it to her. She took it eagerly while Malinche danced in front of her. She pulled back her right arm and threw the ball as hard as she could. It didn't go far, but Malinche didn't care. She raced to the ball, scooped it up in her mouth and was back to Louisa in seconds.

"Not bad for an old lady. Try it again. You can do it."

I looked over at Louisa to see if she'd taken offense to Malinche's comment about her being an old lady, but she was smiling and didn't seem to care at all. This time Malinche stood in front of her with the ball in her mouth, impatiently waiting while Louisa took the ball and threw it again. This went on for quite a while, and each time Louisa was able to throw the ball farther.

Finally Alba interrupted the game. "Malinche, that's enough for one day. Louisa hasn't done this for a long time and you don't want to tire her.

John plays ball with you every day; it isn't as if you don't ever get to do it. Give it a rest for today."

Malinche, dutiful daughter that she was, dropped the ball and sat quietly at Louisa's side. "That was great, Louisa. You could be pretty good if you practiced."

Louisa ran her hand over Malinche's shiny black coat and agreed. "You're right, sweet girl; it's been too long. I am a little tired though. Maybe Alba is right; let's walk, and then maybe sit over there on that bench.

We walked over to the bench and sat down, both girls sitting as close to Louisa as they could without actually being on her lap. I asked Louisa if she'd like a cup of coffee and when she said she would, I walked across the street to the coffee shop while the girls stayed with Louisa. When I came back, the girls were lying at her feet and she was sound asleep. As I sat down, she opened her eyes and said that she was resting her eyes, but that she was ready for coffee.

While we drank our coffee, I asked Louisa about her house. "Has your home been sold?"

"No. My son and his wife haven't decided what to do with it yet."

"Why is your house their decision? What about what you want to do? It is your house, isn't it?"

"Yes, it's my house. My husband and I built that house forty years ago and I've lived there ever since. It was hard after he died, but it's my home and I couldn't bear to leave it, even though people said that I didn't need a big house anymore. I miss being there, but I don't think my son feels that I can take care of myself any longer."

"What about before you broke your hip, Louisa? Were you taking care of yourself then?"

"Oh yes, I managed fine. I had someone come in to clean once a week, but I prepared my own meals and took care of the dogs. I wasn't much good at chopping wood any more, but a neighbor boy came over and helped out with the wood and other chores."

"I don't mean to intrude on your private life, but it seems to me that once your hip heals, you should be able to go back to your own home."

"And, you should have more dog friends live with you." Alba was listening and wanted to add her opinion. "Malinche and I will come over and visit, but you need to live with dogs. You could go to the shelter and adopt two dogs."

"Yeah, gotta have at least two." Now Malinche was adding her two cents. "We could go with you and help you pick out the perfect ones. Dogs that play ball."

By now, Louisa was wide awake and listening carefully. "Do you actually think I could go back to my own home? I think my son assumes that I'll continue to live at Rainbow Retreat even after my hip is completely healed."

"Is that what you want? It's important that whatever you do is your decision."

"I understand, Dale. Before you and the girls started coming to visit, I didn't care about anything. I didn't care if my hip healed. I didn't care where

I lived. I was so depressed that I was just lying there waiting to die. When my son came to visit, I didn't want to think about my house or anything else. I guess I gave him the impression that he could do whatever he wanted with it."

"Has he been to see you in the last month? Have you talked with him about any of this recently?" Louisa and I had never talked about her family and so I had no idea how often they came to visit or what kind of relationship she had with them. Our visits always centered on the B.G.s and having fun with them.

"Yes, he comes to see me about once a week. And, I've told him about the girls. He's seen the pictures you've put up in my room and he knows they come to visit. But, I haven't dared to bring up the subject of going home because I'm afraid he'll say no."

"Louisa, listen carefully to me. If you're capable of taking care of yourself in your own home, where you go after your hip is healed isn't your son's decision. I'm sure he loves you and wants what's best for you, but it'll be up to you to convince him that he won't have to worry about you if you decide to return home. If he thinks that you're an old lady waiting to die, he won't support your decision to go back home. On the other hand, if you want to live and be happy in your own home, then he needs to know that."

"You're right, Dale. He's coming by tomorrow and so I'll speak to him then. Will you and the girls be with me when I talk to him? I need your moral support."

Before I could answer, both girls gave her big slurps and assured her that we'd all be with her. I wasn't so sure that our being there was a good idea because I didn't want her son to think we were ganging up on him, but Louisa said she was sure he wouldn't mind. She assured me that he was really a nice man and that we'd like him. So, I agreed with the girls and said that we'd join them tomorrow.

Having made our decisions for the day, we walked to the car and drove Louisa back to Rainbow Retreat where we saw her to her room and made sure she was comfortable in bed for the rest of the evening. When we left her, she was smiling and looking at the many pictures I'd taken of her with the B.G.s.

Since the girls were going with me the next day, I called John at work and asked if they could stay for the night. He said he didn't mind because he had a meeting and wouldn't be home until late anyway. The B.G.s were happy to stay and made themselves comfortable for the evening. Alba's arthritis made it difficult for her to climb up on the bed and Malinche never left her side, so they slept close by on the floor, carefully monitored by our three Schnauzers, Pip, Joey and Fitz. Actually, all five dogs are good friends because they've spent so much time together and our guys are always gracious about dog sleep-overs.

The next day we did our usual beach walk and then drove to Rainbow Retreat. Louisa said that her son would be there at about 10:30. I figured if we showed up at 11:00 they would have had some time together before we arrived. When we made our way to Louisa's room, still using the outside entrance, I could see that her son was in the room and they were deep in conversation.

After introductions were made, we all settled down for our talk. Louisa was sitting up in a chair and the girls positioned themselves on either side of her as usual. Louisa's son, Vern, sat on the edge of the bed; I found a folding chair in the closet and sat down to join them.

Louisa jumped right in and said that she and Vern had been talking about the possibility of her going home after her hip healed. She also said that he didn't like the idea because he didn't think she could take care of herself. Vern added that he was worried about her and was afraid that she'd fall again, and he wanted her to be somewhere where she could get help if she needed it. It was clear that Vern loved his mother very much and wanted her to be safe. I could tell that he also thought she was too old and frail to live by herself. After listening to them go back and forth, I finally decided to get involved in the conversation.

"I understand your concerns, Vern, but Louisa tells me that she was doing fine before she fell, and I think it might be important for her to live in her own home. She can wear one of those medical alert monitors at all times. If she needs help, all she has to do is push the button and the paramedics will be there to help her. She can arrange for the person who came to clean to come again once a week. The neighbor boy can continue to do chores for her. She can even get herself set up with Meals on Wheels if she doesn't feel like cooking. I don't see the same woman today that I met a month ago. She's healing well, her spirit is strong, she's gained weight, and regaining her independence seems to be very important to her."

At that point, I thought I'd said enough and didn't want to antagonize him. I could see that Malinche was about to add something, but I looked over at her and shook my head. She got the message and put her paw on Louisa's lap. There's nothing more comforting than getting moral support from a dog. They know how to do it really well. Much better than people.

Vern turned to his mother, told her he loved her and said that he only wanted what was best for her. "I don't want you to be here either, Mom. If you feel that you can take care of yourself at home, I'll talk to your doctor and find out when he thinks you can leave here. Once I have that information, I'll get the house cleaned and ready for you. Is that what you want?"

If Louisa had been up to it, she might have turned cartwheels. She was holding on to both Alba and Malinche so tightly that her knuckles were white. They sat up even straighter and their smiles said it all. "Yes, dear, that's exactly what I want. I'm doing physical therapy every day and so I know I won't need to be here much longer. I feel stronger all the time. Thank you for listening to us."

Vern smiled and shook his head. "It wasn't the listening that convinced me, Mom. I don't know what's been going on with you and these dogs for the past month, but it's watching you with them that has put my mind at ease. I've seen changes in you during the past weeks, and now that I see you with the dogs, I think I understand. They've given you the desire to live and be well. I don't know how, but they have. It's amazing. Are they going to live with you?"

"No, dear. Alba and Malinche already have a home. But, they've promised to come and visit often. I'm going to go to the shelter as soon as I get out of here and adopt two dogs who will be my very own live-in friends."

Two weeks later, Louisa walked out of Rainbow Retreat and went home. Vern had arranged for her house to be cleaned and ready for her, and the girls and I went to visit her on her first night home. She lives in a wonderful old cottage, not far from the beach. The neighbor boy had even been watering and weeding her beautiful flower garden because he knows that she hates to see weeds in her lovely flower beds.

Her home was welcoming, and I think the house had missed her being there as much as she'd missed her familiar surroundings. We sat around her old oak kitchen table and drank coffee while Alba and Malinche wandered around the house, giving Louisa's home their own personal dog inspection. Malinche found an old football under Louisa's bed, and she proudly marched into the kitchen, football in mouth, ready to play.

"This was Rugby's, wasn't it? It tastes like dog. Pretty good."

"Yes, Malinche, that was Rugby's favorite toy. I kept him supplied with old footballs that were no longer used over at the high school. Now that Rugby doesn't need this ball any longer, I guess my new friends could play with it. I'd better keep it, just in case. Rugby would like it if a new friend played with his toy. He always was good at sharing."

"Speaking of new friends, Louisa, when are you going to the shelter? Your home is wonderful, but it seems empty without animal friends."

"You're right, Dale. When I first came home earlier today, I found myself looking for Rugby and Emma. I sat down and had a good cry before I could bear to even do anything. Vern was afraid I was going to be too sad all by myself, but I told him that I needed to grieve for my old friends for a while and then I'd be fine. I'm going to plant a special section in the garden for them. Emma and Rugby always liked to be out in the garden with me and I'm going to plant Forget-Me-Nots in their special place."

Alba came over and put her head in Louisa's lap and looked at her with those wonderful brown eyes. "You know that Emma and Rugby are fine, don't you Louisa? You know they understand."

"Yes, Alba. I do. For a time, after Dale told me that they had died, I felt so guilty for leaving them. I was so sad that I couldn't be with them until the end. But, somehow, without even talking about it, you and Malinche have taught me that they're always with me. I still miss them, of course, but I know that having two new friends will help me. Because I loved Emma and Rugby so much, I can pass that love on to other dogs. My being able to do that will be Rugby and Emma's legacy."

"Well, okay then. When do we go and get your new friends? We've gotta be sure and find dogs that play ball. You have to keep in shape." Malinche was eager, as always, to move on to the next adventure.

"I want to go tomorrow. Will you drive me, Dale? Girls, can you come too? It's so important to me that you all be there, especially my wonderful B.G.s. You've given me a reason to live, and it seems right that you be there to help me pick out my new friends."

The girls and I said that we'd be happy to drive her to the shelter and arranged to pick Louisa up the next day at 1:00. After we'd said our good-byes, the girls and I went back to my place to wait for John. He said that it was fine if the girls went to the shelter but that I'd need to pick them up at his office because it was "Bring Your Dog to the Office" day tomorrow, and he'd be taking them with him in the morning.

The next day I stopped to pick up the girls at John's office before we went to get Louisa. They'd had a fun morning hanging out with John's co-workers and playing with the other dogs that had come to work. When we got to Louisa's house, she was waiting out in the front yard. The shelter wasn't far away and we were there in minutes. When we arrived, I told Louisa that the girls and I would wait for her on the other side of the fence that surrounds the cage area while she walked around in front of the cages and looked at the dogs. That way she could see us and know we were there, but Alba and Malinche's presence wouldn't upset the dogs because they wouldn't be walking with Louisa directly in front of the cages.

I also told her that I'd called the shelter earlier in the morning to tell them that she was coming and Barb, a friend who volunteered there, would take her around to meet the dogs. I suggested that only she and Barb look at the dogs so we wouldn't influence her in any way. The adoption choices needed to be hers alone. I added that she'd know which dogs needed to come home with her. Since she'd adopted Emma from the shelter, she knew exactly what I was saying and agreed to go in alone.

While Louisa went into the shelter, the girls and I went around back and walked on the road that borders the fence enclosing the cage area. All of the dogs at the shelter immediately started barking and carrying on because even though we weren't directly in front of their cages, they could see us from the outside portion of their cages. We walked down the road until we were out of sight; then we stopped at a bench that was placed near the road and I sat down. Alba and Malinche were very quiet.

"Are you girls okay about being here? I know this is an unsettling place and if it's hard for you, we can go back to the car."

They both snugged close to me and reassured me that even though it was hard to see dogs in cages, they knew it was important to Louisa that they be there and they'd be fine. They both added that they felt so fortunate to have a wonderful home and wished the same for the dogs that were at the shelter still waiting to be adopted.

As we enjoyed the sunshine, I held on to my B.G.s, knowing that even as secure as they were, it was nerve wracking for them to be here. Gradually, the girls relaxed, but my eyes never left the road as we waited for Louisa to appear.

I knew that once she made her choices, a volunteer would take Louisa and the two dogs she'd chosen out to meet us. I was so curious and excited for Louisa I could hardly sit still.

After what seemed like a long time, but was probably only about twenty minutes, I saw Louisa and my friend Barb, the volunteer, walking toward us. Louisa had a leash in each hand and at the ends of the leashes were two dogs that looked very much alike- both Lab mixes. There was pure joy in their eyes as the pair looked at Louisa. Even though I knew they must be bursting with energy and delighted to be out of their cages, the two dogs walked nicely with Louisa, measuring their paces to hers.

As they came closer, I could see that Louisa was smiling and talking to the dogs, while Barb walked along with that "Oh boy, these guys are going home" look on her face. I knew that look because I'd worn it on many happy occasions myself when I'd volunteered at the shelter.

As the happy foursome moved toward us, the girls and I were so anxious to meet the new dogs we all stood and quickly walked over to be introduced to them.

What a wonderful greeting took place. Alba and Malinche went right up to the new guys and introduced themselves, while Louisa told us all about them.

"Dale, Alba, Malinche, I want you to meet Socks and Junior. They're father and son. Both of them were found at the side of the road on the south end of the island several weeks ago and were brought to the shelter. They told me they'd been on the run for a week before they were found. They'd escaped from an abusive situation. Junior was limping because he'd been hit by a rock that had been thrown at him, but he's fine now. They said they'd love to come home with me. Aren't they handsome?"

I greeted both dogs, running my hands over their skinny bodies. They weren't exactly handsome yet, but with love, good food and a safe home they would be soon. "Hi guys. It's a pleasure to meet you. You're going to have a wonderful home with Louisa."

Both dogs smiled and pressed as close to Louisa as they could without knocking her over. Socks was the first to speak.

"Hi, it's nice to meet you too. Junior and I took one look at this nice lady when she stood in front of our cage and knew she was the one. We've been waiting for her."

"Yeah, we've been waiting," Junior added. "When can we go home? It's so noisy here."

Louisa asked Barb if Socks and Junior could come home with her right away, and Barb said that they certainly could, as soon as the paperwork was completed. I told Louisa to go on in and take care of the adoption details while the girls and I took the new guys to the car.

I walked the dogs to the car while Louisa went into the office. Socks, Junior and the B.G.s all climbed in the back seat while I stood outside. It was crowded for them, but they all sorted themselves out as dogs can do while we waited for Louisa.

Out she came, new leashes and collars in hand. She'd purchased a bright red collar and matching leash for Socks, which would look great with his black and white coloring, and a bright blue set for Junior who was mostly brown, with a few white markings here and there. As she got in the car, Socks and Junior draped themselves over the top of her seat and gave her noisy kisses and slurps.

They understood that they couldn't climb up onto her lap, but I knew that's what they wanted to do. Both dogs showed admirable restraint.

The ride back to Louisa's house was filled with noisy chatter from the dogs as well as from Louisa. Malinche talked about playing ball with Socks; Alba was being solicitous of Junior, and Louisa told me all about how she'd chosen the guys.

"I walked in front the kennels while your friend Barb told me about each dog. Naturally, I wanted to take all of them home, but I knew I couldn't, so I tried to keep an open mind and wait for some kind of a signal. As it turned out, Socks and Junior were the last dogs we saw. When I stood in front of their kennel, they immediately came up to the gate and each of them reached a paw through the kennel wire. I took one look at them and knew they were my dogs. I didn't care who they were, what their story was, how old they were, or even what they looked like. I just knew. And they did too. They both sat, quietly, smiling at me. We stood for the longest time holding hands and paws and looking at each other. Barb was amazed because she said that usually they were noisy and jumpy when people came by to see them. I could have adopted any dogs I saw, but these two wonderful boys chose me and I chose them back."

Louisa, Socks and Junior are a family now. The boys, as Louisa calls them, have gained weight and their coats are shiny and thick. They both sleep on the bed with her, and all three go for walks each day and on nice days they all work in the garden. The Forget-Me-Nots planted in memory of Rugby and Emma are thriving as is Louisa's relationship with the boys. The B.G.s and I come by often and the four dogs have fun playing together while Louisa and I visit. I know that Alba and Malinche have talked to the boys about how they met Louisa because Socks and Junior clearly understand the importance of Louisa's relationship with the B.G.s. The boys defer to the girls and are always happy to strut their stuff when we all come to visit. They're anxious to have Alba and Malinche understand that they're taking very good care of their lady.

Yesterday after we left Louisa and the boys, Alba and Malinche both gave contented sighs as I drove them back to John's house. I gave a sigh that matched theirs and was smiling to myself when I heard two wonderful dog voices from the back seat.

"So, Dale, what about that lady named Annie who you told us about? Think we ought to visit her?"

"I wonder if she plays ball … "

Siam Brave heart

Her coat was so matted and dirty I could barely tell there was a dog under that horrible mess. Twigs, dirt clods, weeds and burrs were firmly embedded in her fur. Huge thick mats and heavy tangles hung all over her body. I needed to be closer to her, so I opened the door to her cage and went inside.

"Hey, my friend. How're you doing?"

She was leaning against the side of the cage, facing away from me and didn't respond to the sound of my voice. She didn't see or hear me until I kneeled down and gently touched her back. Then she turned and her cloudy eyes barely focused on me. "Oh, sorry, I didn't see you. Have you come to help me?"

"Absolutely. That's why I'm here. What's your name, my girl?"

"I'm Siam. Could you please sit on the floor so I can lean on you? I'm so tired."

"I'd love to sit with you. I'll get a blanket and be right back."

I went into the animal shelter office, found a blanket and hurried back to Siam's cage. Now she was standing close to the front of the cage, waiting for me. I went inside, spread the blanket down on the cold concrete, sat down and drew her to me. She collapsed on my lap and let out a huge sigh.

"That's better. Thank you. I'm not sure where I am and because I don't see well, I keep running into the walls. You're nice and soft."

I could hardly stand the smell of her, but I didn't even think about moving away. While I stroked her tangled fur I tried to hold down the anger I felt toward whoever had allowed her to become so matted and dirty. I knew that being angry with some nameless person wouldn't be of any help to Siam right now, so I pushed my anger aside and tried to concentrate on sending her as much positive energy as I could generate.

She scrunched around so she could look at me. "I know I smell bad. I'm sorry, but there isn't anything I can do about it. Maybe you could give me a bath?"

"I'd love to give you a bath. But, I think it's going to take more than a bath to make you feel better. I may have to cut some of your hair off too. Is that okay with you?"

"Sure, whatever it takes. I'm not very comfortable. But then, I haven't been for a long time. Do you know where I am and why I'm here? Did I do something wrong?"

"You're at the animal shelter, but I don't know why you're here. If you'd like, I can go back to the office and find out how you got here."

"Yes, please. But, not right now. I like sitting here with you. Your hands feel good and I like being touched."

So, we sat together for a while. I sang to her and bless her heart, she didn't seem to mind that I have a terrible voice. She sank deeper and deeper into my lap. Finally, I heard snores and realized she was fast asleep. It was clear that she was exhausted and so after I made sure that she was comfortable on the blanket, I gently eased away from her and went to the office to find out what I could about this badly neglected dog.

The person on duty in the office found Siam's paperwork and told me that she had been brought in about an hour ago by a neighbor of the man who had been her human companion. He couldn't care for her any longer because he was ill. Apparently there hadn't ever been any care because the information on the surrender papers indicated that she had been chained up in the backyard her whole life.

"How old is she?"

"Well, let's see. It says here that she's fourteen."

Oh, no. No wonder she looks like she does. If she's been chained up in a backyard for fourteen years, that explains everything. How can people be so cruel?

"Thanks for the information. I'm going to see what I can do to make her more comfortable. It'll probably take a few days because I need to get rid of the mats and tangles before I bathe her."

"No problem. She isn't going anywhere. Chows are hard to adopt and because she's so old, probably no one will want her. We may end up euthanizing her to put her out of her misery, but that decision won't be made for a while so feel free to do what you can for her."

I'd heard enough to give me the picture, so I went back outside to see how Siam was doing. She was still sound asleep. I found a few more blankets and moved to the inside of her cage to set up a warm place for her on the plastic platform that would serve as her bed. After I had built a nest with the blankets, I crawled through the doggie door to the outside part of her cage where she was sleeping on the blanket I had brought in with me earlier.

I gently picked her up and carried her around to the inside and laid her on her bed. In spite of her heavy coat, I could feel her ribs and every bone along her back. She was painfully thin under all that mess of a coat.

She stirred, but didn't wake up until I was fussing with her blankets to be sure she was warm and comfortable. "Oh, it's you. Hi. I feel warmer now. This is nice. Did you find out about me?"

"Yes, I have some information, but it isn't important right now. The best thing for you to do would be to rest, get a good night's sleep, and I'll come back to see you tomorrow. Are you hungry?"

"No, I'm fine. I'm so tired I can hardly keep my eyes open. What's your name? I should know it, but I'm feeling so tired I can't see it."

"My name's Dale."

"Okay, Dale. You'll come back tomorrow?"

"I sure will, Siam. I'll be back tomorrow; we'll go for a walk and then we can get started on cleaning you up. Sleep well, my friend. I'll dream with you tonight."

That was the beginning of my friendship with Siam the Chow. Every day for a week I went back to the shelter and spent time with her. The job of cleaning her up looked impossible at first, but each day I was able to get rid of more and more mats and tangles. Brushing didn't work at all, so I had to actually shave much of her fur off to get rid of the dirty mess and give her skin a chance to breathe. She was so patient. I'd work for a while and then walk with her to give her a break.

At first when we walked she was wobbly, but as the grooming progressed, her step became livelier and I knew she felt better.

Finally the day came when I could actually bathe her. The mats and tangles were gone, and even though her body was shaved pretty closely, I'd managed to preserve some of the fur on her legs and around her head so she didn't look too strange.

"Okay, my girl. Today is bath day. You're going to like this. The water is nice and warm, and we won't go back outside until you're dry. Up you go."

I lifted her up into the bathtub, adjusted the water so it was warm and off we went. She stood there with her eyes closed enjoying the warmth of the water on her body. "Oh, this feels good. I don't think I've ever had a bath."

The water that ran off of her was black. Filthy. I've bathed lots of dogs, but I'd never seen anything like this. It took three shampooings that day to get her reasonably clean. I knew we had more work to do on her coat, but I thought three shampoos in one day were probably enough for the first time. After her bath, I wrapped her in a big warm towel and sat in the office with her until she was dry. Because it was cold outside and the cages weren't heated during the day, and not even at night until the temperature dropped to below thirty degrees, I rigged up a sweatshirt for her to wear so she wouldn't be too cold. Then I found a red bandanna and wrapped it around her neck. Just for effect.

"Hey, sweetheart, you look pretty cute. Are you comfortable?"

"What am I wearing? I didn't think dogs wore clothes. It feels funny. Warm though."

"No, dogs don't usually wear clothes, but it's cold and I've had to shave off so much of your fur I thought maybe the sweatshirt would help keep you warm. Do you feel too embarrassed to wear it?"

"Oh, no. I feel clean, thanks. A little naked, but I guess my fur will grow. It's good to not be so dirty. Do I smell better?"

"You smell like strawberries. Wonderful. You're beautiful, you know. Quite a stunning lady."

And so it went. Weeks went by and there were more baths. More grooming. Finally her coat started to shine and her beautiful mahogany color gleamed. The part I'd had to shave gradually grew in and felt fuzzy, like puppy fur. Our walks became longer and she almost pranced when she walked. She still didn't hear or see well, but I knew she felt better.

During our walks and time together, we talked and I learned that she had indeed been chained outside for her entire life. She didn't know that there was any other way to live. When I asked her about her human companion, she smiled a kind of sad smile and said that she guessed he hadn't known any better. She had come to him when she was a puppy and had never been inside his house. I had explained to her early on why she was at the shelter and she understood. She said, in that infinitely wise way dogs have of knowing what's true, that she was sorry she hadn't been allowed to be of more help to her person.

After a couple of months, I noticed that Siam was becoming restless in her cage. She was more comfortable than she'd ever been, but she felt well enough to want to spend more and more time walking and being outside. She loved being in the office, watching the action, greeting people, letting people pet her, and enjoying the company.

One day when we were walking, we stopped to rest at a bench out on the trail. I sat on the bench and she sat in front of me with her head on my lap. The day was sunny and we both were snoozing lazily in the sun, enjoying the warmth.

"Siam, my dear friend. I wish I could take you to my house with me. I hate leaving you here when I know that you deserve to live in a real home with someone who will love you and appreciate what a wonderful dog you are."

"That's a kind thought, Dale, but that's not what our relationship is all about. Besides, there's somewhere else I need to be for a while. It's time you looked for my place."

So, we began doing just that. I did a little write up about her, which I put on the outside of her cage, and we started putting her picture (very cute with T-shirt and red bandanna) in the local papers with the hope that someone would see it and come to adopt her.

Weeks after the search began, I arrived at the shelter one day and I was told that a woman had called about Siam and was coming to see her that afternoon. I was like a little kid. Excited. Hopeful. Full of questions. "Who is it? Does she sound like she's really interested? Will she provide a good home for her? When's she coming?"

The staff person who had the information about the call only knew that the woman had a Chow friend that had died recently and when she saw Siam's picture in the paper, she felt that she had to come and see her. She hadn't said what time she was coming, only that she'd come by with her mother to take a look at Siam.

When I went out to Siam's cage, I wanted to tell her about the woman, but I didn't want to get her hopes up if she never came, or, if she didn't like Siam. I couldn't imagine anyone not liking her, but then I was hardly objective when it came to this marvelous dog so I said nothing. Or, so I thought.

"Dale, relax. It's going to be fine. You'll see."

I knew better than to question her because dogs are so intuitive that she had obviously picked up on my excitement. And, it was clear that she knew more than I did … always. So, we went for our walk, and hung out in the exercise yard for a while. Waiting. She was patient; I was pretending unsuccessfully that it was just an ordinary day.

Finally, about 3:00 two women came out to the exercise yard and introduced themselves. They were the ones! I let them into the area, closed the gate, and stood aside while the two women went over to Siam.

Siam felt them coming, walked over and stood quietly in front of the youngest woman who had introduced herself as Edith. Edith kneeled in front of Siam and held her head in both hands. They stayed that way for what seemed an interminable length of time while Edith talked quietly and Siam's tail waved gently back and forth. The older woman, Edith's mother, Janet, talked to me, but I didn't really hear anything she said. I was so focused on Edith and Siam that I knew I was just making polite conversation, not paying much attention to her. I wanted to go over to Siam and Edith and talk to them, but I knew I had to stay out of it.

Finally, Edith stood up, turned to me, and said, "I'd like to adopt Siam." Just like that. I hadn't realized that I was holding my breath, but when it all came out in one big whoosh, I knew that I'd been doing an anticipatory shallow breath thing that wasn't allowing much air to get into my lungs.

I looked at Siam, who calmly walked over to me and gave my arm a little tug with her paw. That's what she did when she wanted me to bend down and talk to her.

"Okay, my girl. Is she the one?"

"Yes, Dale. She's the one. It's time for me to go."

I stood up and talked with Edith and Janet while Siam listened (not so much with her ears because she couldn't hear in that way) intently at my side. I told them about Siam's history, how wonderful she was, what her health was like, her age, what I felt her needs were, and in general I was the ultimate overprotective parent. Edith talked about the death of her Chow friend, how much she missed her, and what a great companion she thought Siam would be for her. She didn't seem bothered by Siam's age or her inability to see and hear well, and said that her other friend had been sixteen when she died. She assured me that she had a large fenced yard, but that Siam would live in the house with her. She was horrified to hear about Siam's life at the end of a chain and reassured me that her life would be different now.

After talking with Edith, I felt that this was Siam's chance to live a better life, for however long that would be. I excused myself and went into the office to recommend to shelter staff that Edith be allowed to adopt Siam. Staff would have questions for her as well as paperwork to fill out, so I went back outside and told Edith and Janet to go in and take care of the paperwork while I stayed with Siam.

After the women went inside, Siam and I went over to the wooden bench that sits near the fence and I picked her up and held her on my lap. She had gained enough weight so the effort wasn't easy, but we managed. After we were settled, I wrapped my arms around her and laid my head next to hers. I had no words, but even if I had wanted to talk, I couldn't have conjured up the words because my tears made it impossible for me to speak. I felt so happy for her, but I knew that I would miss her.

"It's okay, Dale. Don't cry. I have work to do with Edith, but we'll see each other again. Don't worry. I love you. We can still dream together."

I dried my tears on the sleeve of my sweatshirt, and we got up and went into the office. Edith was finishing up with the paperwork, and shelter employees were standing behind the counter smiling and giving enthusiastic thumbs up signs to me. Edith had brought a collar and leash, which I attached to Siam while the last of the adoption papers were signed, and then we walked out to Edith's car.

When we got to the car, Siam jumped in, turned around and gave me a big grin and a very sloppy kiss. Edith got in and shut the door as she turned to me and said, "Don't worry. I'll take good care of her."

And then they drove away.

After Siam had been gone a few days, I wanted to call Edith and see how things were going, but volunteers weren't allowed to contact adopters and so I resisted the inclination. I continued to send Siam positive thoughts and hopes that her new home was working out well for her. We did dream together, and she felt happy in my dreams, so I stopped worrying and waited for news to come from a follow-up call by the shelter.

Finally, after a week, someone at the shelter called to see how Siam was doing, and the reports were good. Edith loved her. Siam seemed happy. All was well.

About a month or so later, the local paper did a piece on happy endings, and Siam's picture appeared in the paper. She was leaning against

Edith, looking like a happy dog. I was delighted, relieved and pleased for both Siam and Edith. I love a happy ending.

Many months later I came to the shelter on one of my regular days of volunteering, and when I went into the office to sign in, the staff person on duty greeted me with a very serious face. Uh oh. She was about to tell me something I didn't want to hear.

"Hi Dale. I hate to be the one to tell you this, but Siam's back. She's in her old kennel."

Now, I have to tell you that when you spend enough time around an animal shelter, you get used to the idea (well, not really) that some dogs are returned after a period of time. The excuses are always the same: not housebroken, doesn't get along with the other dog, barks too much, chases cats, or "We're moving and can't take the dog." I'd become accustomed to the "rent-a-dog" syndrome where people adopt an animal and then aren't willing to take the time or have the patience to help the dog adjust. Or they move and the dog becomes dispensable.

But, I never ever thought I'd see Siam back at the shelter. Never.

I was incredulous. "Why? Why is she back? What happened?"

The answer floored me. "Well, the lady's husband came home from sea duty and he didn't want Siam in the house, so he put her out in the yard, but she barked all the time. He brought her back this morning."

My thoughts all ran together. Edith's husband? Her husband? What was I hearing? She never said she had a husband. Oh, no. I never thought to ask. My fault. She didn't talk like she had a husband. How could she let this happen?

I raced outside and went to Siam's cage, hoping that it wasn't true. I didn't want to see her in there. Please, let it not be true.

But it was. My beautiful friend was standing there, behind bars again, looking at me with those cloudy eyes, head slightly cocked. Patient as always. "Hi Dale."

I couldn't get inside the cage fast enough. "Siam. Siam. Are you all right? I'm so sorry to see you here. I thought everything was going well. I didn't know that Edith had a husband. Why did he put you outside? How could he not like you? I never wanted you to be banished outside again. I'm so sorry; please forgive me. I didn't ask enough questions. Or, I didn't ask the right questions."

I was holding her, blathering like an idiot. Siam waited for me to sputter out before she finally said, "Look Dale, it's okay. Edith needed me to help her grieve for her other animal friend. I gave her what she needed and now my work is finished. Please don't be upset. I'm happy to see you."

"I'm happy to see you too, dearheart. But, I didn't want to see you here. C'mon, let's go for a walk."

We walked and talked, and I noticed that she limped, but when I asked her about the limp, she said it was nothing and not to worry. I felt so awful when I had to bring her back to her cage. She was beautiful, though. Her coat had grown in, luxurious and thick. Edith had obviously taken good physical care of her because there were no mats or tangles, a sure sign that she'd been brushed on a regular basis. And, she was well fed. But, she was back at the shelter. I hated that.

When I left the shelter that day I had a really strong urge to call Edith to rant and rave at her about Siam, but I didn't. What's done is done. If she had allowed her husband to bring Siam back to the shelter, then she obviously didn't want her any more. Her loss. I was angry and frustrated, but people get to make choices and it was none of my business. How cruel that the choices people make affect animals in such a devastating way. I forced myself to remember what Siam had said to me about her work with Edith being done and that she knew why being with her was right, even if for a short time. Replaying Siam's words in my head didn't help though; I still felt so sad.

I was gone all the next day, but when I came home there was a message on my answering machine from the volunteer coordinator at the shelter. Siam wasn't doing well. Could I please come and see her?

It was early evening and the shelter was closed, but I knew that the volunteer coordinator- a woman who was tireless in her efforts to help the animals- would still be there so I jumped in my car and went right over.

"What's wrong with Siam?"

"It looks like her back end has given out. She can't walk. She hardly moved all day. Would you go out and take a look? Maybe you can get her up"

I went out to Siam's cage and found her lying on her blanket. Head on her paws. Not sleeping, just staring. Waiting.

I went inside and sat down on the blanket with her. "Hey, my friend. What's wrong?"

"Oh, hi Dale; I'm glad you're here. I can't walk anymore. It's time for me to go Home. Will you help me, please?"

"Oh, Siam, my braveheart. Are you sure it's time? Maybe if you came to my house with me, I could take care of you."

"Yes, Dale, I'm sure. My work is finished and I can't stay here any longer. No, I can't come to your house. It's time for me to move on. You understand; I know you do."

I did understand. I didn't like it, but I understood. With a promise that I'd help her, I went back into the shelter and talked with the volunteer co-ordinator. She listened to what I had to say and said that she'd talk with the shelter manager and hopefully an appointment could be made soon with the local vet who would help Siam leave her body.

The next morning I received a call letting me know that the appointment had been made for that afternoon. I went to the shelter early so I could spend time with Siam before we went to the vet. She couldn't walk at all, so I carried her around, and we spent a quiet hour in an empty office waiting for the time to pass. Siam was calm as always and she assured me that she was fine and would be dancing in a short while.

When it was time, I carried her to the van and held her on my lap as the shelter staff person drove to the vet. Once there, we brought her in and I wrapped my arms around her as she was given the injection that would send her on her way.

Siam died with quiet dignity, just as she had lived this life. As I felt her slip away, I gave silent thanks that she had been a part of my life. I wished her well and thanked her for all she had taught me. I told her that I loved her … and I let her go.

That night we dreamed together- my Siam and I. She was right. She was dancing. She was healthy, happy, and content. I danced with her and saw in her wholeness a truly marvelous presence.

Siam Braveheart, you are very well loved.

Thank you, my friend.

Diana's Gang

Shady, Maxie, Boo Boo, Otto, Duncan, McKenna, Foxy and Blue all raced toward me like some kind of mismatched dog herd. As I worked to unlatch the gate, all of the dogs clamored to be heard while Diana nonchalantly walked behind them. Once I stepped inside the yard, Shady almost knocked me over in her enthusiasm, while the others milled around in a wonderful tail wagging blur, barking and shouting their hellos as loudly as they could.

"Okay guys, I hear you. Hi, everybody. How're you all doing?"

"Hi, Dale." "Got any cookies?" "Pet me." "Play with me." "Where's the chewy you said you'd bring?" "C'mon in." "Let's talk." "How about some tug of war?"

The happy energy of Diana's gang was irresistible, as always, and I quickly began handing out cookies, greeting them all, being so glad I was there to visit. Surrounded by a happy, rowdy dog herd was like receiving a transfusion of pure joy. Diana stood back, smiling, as I greeted each of her eight dog friends.

Diana is a rescuer. Over the years, she's adopted at least thirty dogs from various shelters and rescue organizations. She always takes the "hard cases"- dogs that are old, need medication, are hard to manage, or have been at the shelter for a long time and are considered unadoptable. The walls of her modest home are covered with photographs of dogs she has loved that have discovered happiness with her. There are even several beautiful portraits of dogs that Diana painted herself, though she's quick to point out that she isn't an artist. If you're a dog, finding a home with Diana is like winning the dog lotto.

I'd met Diana when I was told that Shady, a Lab/Rottweiler mix, had been adopted by her. Shady is a special friend that I'd met at the shelter, and when she was there, Shady was anxious, frightened and unhappy. She had been brought in with her brother, on whom she was very dependent, but he was adopted quickly because he was healthy and outgoing, while Shady was skinny and shy. Shady was sad and lonely without his support. It was so wonderful to see how she thrived in her new home, and I visited her and the rest of the gang as often as I could. When Diana had to be gone for more than a couple of hours, which was the self imposed limit of time that she felt comfortable being away from her gang, I came over and stayed with them.

"Hey, Dale. Guess what?" Shady called out to me. "I get to sleep on the bed with my new friend. I get lots to eat. Maxie and I play all the time. I love it here. I'm so glad to see you."

"Hi, Shady, my girl. You look better every time I see you. Your coat shines, and I can't see your ribs any more. Best of all, you're smiling! I didn't see too many smiles at the shelter."

"Yeah, I look great, don't I? C'mon inside."

Diana finally got a word in to say hello and to welcome me. She's a shy, reclusive lady who isn't in the best of health, but she and the gang take care of each other. Until recently, she shared her home with her mother, but Mom died a short time ago and now the responsibility (although she wouldn't call it that) of caring for the dogs falls solely on Diana. When people ask her how she manages, she simply responds that the dogs are her life. Because of her health problems, she knows that eventually she'll need help on a regular basis, but she always says that she'll cross that bridge when the time comes.

With all eight exuberant guys at our heels, we went inside. Going into Diana's house is accomplished by either going up the few steps to the front door or walking up a ramp that she'd had built several years ago for a dog named Scout that couldn't manage stairs. Diana went into the kitchen to make coffee while I sat on the floor, surrounded by furry bodies. Shady, as usual, barged her way into the center of the group and draped herself all over me.

"C'mon, Shady. Let me spend some time with the rest of the gang too. Don't be so pushy."

"Pushy? Me? You know you love it. Besides, the rest of these guys don't know you as well as I do. I get special attention, don't I?"

"Special attention, sure. Always. But, I'd like to talk to the others too."

With a grin of understanding, Shady bounded over to Maxie, a large Bernese/Australian Shepherd mix, and started to play with her. (Maxine seems too formal a name for this enthusiastic big girl, so Diana calls her Maxie.) Maxie and Shady had become instant best friends when Diana first brought Shady to her house, and they never tire of the special games they play with each other. I don't think either of them had the opportunity to play much before they came to Diana's house and they're obviously making up for lost time. It was fun to watch them, but my attention was soon diverted by Foxy, a beautiful tan Greyhound/Lab mix. (All of the dogs are mixes of some sort.) Foxy leaned into me and put her head on my shoulder.

"Hi, Dale. It's nice to see you again."

"And you, lovely lady. How's life for you today?"

"Oh, it's good. Really good. It's cold outside, but we've been in, lying around near the wood stove and so I feel warm and safe. I spent all my time outside before I came to Diana, and I can't seem to get enough of being inside a warm house."

"Well, m'dear, you certainly deserve to be warm and safe. I'm so glad you're here."

While Foxy and I had our love-in, Otto and Boo Boo hovered nearby waiting their turn for attention. Both dogs are Shepherd/Husky mixes and they hang out together. Their gentle ways are so endearing. Even though they're senior members of the gang, they patiently wait their turn when someone comes to visit. Everyone learns to share at Diana's house.

Foxy moved aside as I reached with both arms for Otto and Boo Boo. "Hey you two, come closer so I can snug with you." No further encouragement needed, both of them moved in closer and I received kisses from each of them. They stood quietly while I ran my hands over their thick coats. At that moment, I truly felt like I had an animal heart. Otto nuzzled closer and smiled his approval of my feelings. He whispered, "Enjoy the moment, Dale," before he moved away so I could greet the Sheltie duo.

McKenna and Duncan are Shelties, a favorite breed of Diana's. The little Shelties do a wonderful job of keeping their distance from the bigger dogs, while still maintaining their positions in the pack. Of this particular gang of eight, McKenna has been there the longest. He's an older guy too and doesn't see or hear well. His role as Diana's "protector" is understood by the rest of the dogs and they allow him the space he needs. He spends most of his time in Diana's bedroom, comfortable and secure in his own little world. Duncan is more outgoing, and he welcomed my touch, while Mc Kenna graciously allowed a quick pat before he darted back to Diana's side.

Blue, an Australian Shepherd, was the last to come over and sit with me. She'd been shy with me the first few times I'd come to visit, but now she was as welcoming as the rest of the gang. "Hey, Dale. What's up?"

"Hi, Miss Blue. Not much. Just came by for a visit. You're looking beautiful today. And you smell like you had a bath. I don't suppose you took care of the grooming yourself?"

"Yeah, sure, that'll be the day. Diana brushed me and gave me a bath yesterday. She did both Maxie and me and it took her almost all day. I worry about her sometimes because we're a lot of work, but she doesn't seem to mind and she knows we like to be brushed and stuff. She's such a great lady."

By now, Diana had come into the living room with coffee for both of us. I drank mine, with dogs sprawled near me, while she had hers in her favorite chair, with McKenna and Blue stationed on either side of her. Just drinking coffee was uneventful with this crew, in contrast to times when cake was served and I would try to eat cake and play keep-away with eight dogs that tried to convince me they were starving. Fat chance! As I watched the gang, so comfortable and loved in their home, I couldn't help but think of all the neglected and unloved dogs everywhere that might never experience this kind of life. When I had these thoughts I was always thankful for the rescuers among us.

I stayed to visit awhile, enjoying the company of these eight charming dogs and their gentle lady, and then took my leave, promising to come again soon. Diana is reclusive, and values her privacy, but she always welcomes me, as do her animal friends.

About a week or so after the visit I've described, Diana called, asking if I'd come over later in the day to help her introduce a new dog to the rest of the gang. One of the volunteers at the animal shelter had told her about an older Sheltie that needed a home; she knew that Diana couldn't resist a Sheltie. After Diana picked him up from the shelter, she was going to take him to her vet to have him checked out, and she wanted me to meet her at her house to help with the introductions. This was something that she and her mother had always done together, and so I was happy to help because it was a two-person job.

I arrived at the house before Diana and was inside playing with the gang when she pulled up with Xander, the newest member of the family. We decided that I'd stay out in the yard with Xander, while she brought the others out, one at a time, so they could do their greetings.

The introductions went smoothly. One by one, the gang came out, sniffed Xander, wagged tails, made their welcoming noises, and went off to play. He was delighted to meet everyone, and before long all of them were out in the yard, roaming around like it was just another day. Xander literally pranced from one dog to the other, tail wagging like crazy. Even Shady, "The Boss," as Diana's mother used to call her, greeted him cheerfully.

"You guys are wonderful! You did such a great job of welcoming Xander. I'm impressed."

They all had something to say. "Why wouldn't we?" "He needs to be here." "He's okay, as long as he doesn't want my food." "He's cool." "He looks like me except that nobody brushed him." "He'll probably wanna sleep on the bed." "We know how to share; it'll be fine."

Diana was happy with the meeting and we all trooped inside for some treats. Except Xander. Xander was reluctant to come in because he'd been tied up outside in his previous home, so he stood on the porch, peeking around the corner of the front door. He looked like he wanted to be inside, so I went out to get him.

"Hey, Xander. C'mon in. You don't have to stay outside here. You belong to a family now and you get to be in the house."

"Really? Wow, that's a change. Are you sure it's okay that I come in? I do want to be with the rest of the gang, but I'm used to being left outside. What's it like in there?"

"It's nice. You can go out anytime you like, but you'll live in the house, along with everyone else."

"All right, if you say so. Let's go."

Once in the house, he started exploring, but when he saw that the rest of the crew were all lined up at the cookie box, he got right in line with everyone else. Diana handed out treats and everyone settled down while Xander continued his exploring. After he'd visited every room, he came into the living room and settled down at Diana's feet, like he'd always been there. What a great sight.

I stayed a bit longer to visit and then took off, knowing that all was well. Before I left, I asked Diana where she thought Xander would sleep that night.

"Probably on my bed with his head on my pillow."

Absolutely right. When I called the next day to see how things were going, Diana reported that Xander, Foxy and Shady had all slept on her bed.

She's perfected the Egyptian Mummy style of sleeping and is quite used to sharing her bed with her canine friends.

As the months passed, Diana's dogs continued to thrive, but Diana knew that she had more than enough room- in both her heart and house- and that it might be time to welcome another dog into the gang.

Enter Thomas.

Thomas had been at the local shelter for several months and even though he was a big, lovable guy, a Golden Retriever mix, people continually overlooked him because he had a skin condition that no one wanted to bother treating. I'd told Diana about seeing his picture in the paper; she made a call to the shelter and a few days later she called to ask if I'd like to come over and meet Thomas.

Thomas had been brought to Diana's house by two volunteers from the shelter who had a special relationship with him and wanted to see him settled in his new home. As with Xander, the gang welcomed him immediately and he was there to stay. By the time I got there later the same day that he'd arrived, he acted like he'd always lived there and came running to welcome me right along with the rest of the gang.

"Hey, Thomas. How're ya doing buddy? Like it here?"

"Hi Dale. What's not to like? This is a great place. I'm gonna love it here!"

And he does. With time, love and a healthy diet, Thomas's skin condition has cleared up and he's a beautiful, healthy dog now. Diana calls him her "psychic" dog because he always knows when someone's coming, usually about five or ten minutes before they arrive. He's devoted to Diana, as are the rest of the gang, and he's found a wonderful home.

Just recently, a puppy mill operation was raided by the animal control authorities, and seventy-one dogs living in unspeakable conditions were rescued and taken to various shelters in the area. Most of the dogs were Shelties and because Diana maintains regular contact with the Sheltie rescue organization, they called and asked if she'd take one of the dogs. The question was a no brainer for her; and so, not long ago, Wadie joined the gang.

When I went over to meet him, Wadie did come out to greet me, but he was shy and his voice was soft and tentative, as is often true with dogs that have been neglected or abused.

"Hi Wadie. It's so nice to see you here. Are you doing okay?"

"Hi." He was whispering so I had to bend down really close to hear him. "You haven't come to take me away, have you?" His voice was barely audible, but his anxiety came through loud and clear.

"Not on your life! I've come to welcome you to your forever home. You don't need to be afraid any more. You'll be safe and loved here."

Wadie was in terrible shape when he arrived and so after a week of special TLC, Diana took him to her vet to be neutered and checked out. After a day of neutering, rotten teeth removal, and various other surgical indignities, Wadie was able to return home and is now doing fine. After spending all of his four years chained outside, serving only as a breeding machine for the puppy mill owner, this little guy now sleeps on the bed and never leaves Diana's side.

And so, as of this moment, Diana and her gang are alive and well. Diana's health is fragile, but her spirit is strong and the need to care for her guys motivates her to do what she can to stay healthy. With so much love in the house, it would be hard to be ill for any length of time. Animal energy is healing and gives strength.

Oh, I forgot to mention the sign that hangs on Diana's gate. The message is clear.

> THIS PROPERTY IS MAINTAINED
> FOR THE COMFORT AND
> SECURITY OF OUR ANIMALS. IF
> YOU DON'T LIKE THAT, PLEASE
> GO AWAY.

Jenny

Deliverance meets Tobacco Road. What a creepy place.

After bumping down a dirt road that was more ruts than pavement, we drove into the yard of a house that looked like it had just barely survived years of neglect. The front porch was hanging by a few nails, windows were broken and boarded up on the house, and there were so many garbage bags filled with who knows what lying around that it was difficult to even see the house. But, what we did see in the yard was appalling.

Four large skinny dogs were chewing on bones and muscle that could only have come from the deer carcass piled in a heap by the front door. The carcass had been gutted and dressed, and the dogs were obviously indulging in leftovers. What kind of a place was this?

I got out of the truck and walked past the dogs. They were so thin that I didn't begrudge them their meal, even though I felt sickened by what I was seeing. Poor guys. I wanted to grab them, put them in the truck and take them away, but unfortunately I hadn't come for them. I'd come for another dog.

A few days earlier we'd received a call from a friend who told us about a Schnauzer whose human companion had died and apparently no one wanted her. I called the number we were given and told the woman who answered that we'd be happy to welcome the dog into our home. The woman didn't speak English very well, and I was unable to get any particulars about the dog except where she could be found. We'd come to this horrible place to bring her home with us. The woman had referred to the dog as "she," so I knew that much at least. It didn't matter whether the dog was male or female; we only knew that the dog needed a home, and we were happy to provide one for her.

I knocked on the door, hoping it wouldn't fall off before someone answered. Finally, after standing there for what seemed like forever, I heard someone open the door. "Yeah?" The man who answered had obviously been asleep and he was rubbing his eyes and scratching his stomach.

"Hi. We've come for the Schnauzer."

Blank look.

"I spoke to someone on the phone yesterday. I said that we'd be happy to take the dog. I think I talked with your wife." I felt like I was giving clues in some bizarre guessing game and found myself shouting to make myself heard over the cacophony of the dogs in the yard.

"Oh, yeah. I'll get her."

Another wait, but finally he returned carrying a dog bed in one arm and a dog in the other.

"Here. You can have her bed too. All she does is sleep so she won't be any trouble."

With those words of enlightenment, he handed me the dog, threw the bed down on the porch and went back inside. Any thoughts I had about asking questions were lost with the slamming of the door. Okay, fine.

I took one look at the dog bed, which was nothing more than a broken down wicker basket with a filthy blanket thrown inside, and left it sitting on the porch. They could add it to their garbage collection. We'd get her a new bed.

As I walked back to the truck, I held the little one as close as I could and talked to her. "Hey, sweetie. You don't need to shake. You're safe now. You're coming home with us." She didn't respond to my words at all, and I could feel that she was terribly thin. No matter, she'd be home soon enough.

Before I got in the truck, I turned to the big dogs. "So sorry big guys. We can't take you with us, but I'll make a call and see if I can't get you out of here. Hang in there."

I handed the little one, who hadn't made a sound, to Ellaine, who was waiting in the passenger seat. Without a word, I started the truck and we left.

After we got back on the main road, I pulled over so we could take a closer look at our new friend before we continued on our way. The dog had stopped shaking, but she was tense and clearly apprehensive.

"Hey, little one. Are you okay?"

No response.

"You're safe now. We're taking you home with us."

As we talked to her, we both were touching her, rubbing her back and head, hoping to elicit some kind of response. The dog burrowed deeper into Ellaine's lap without acknowledging our presence in any way. The only communication we picked up was a very very faint message that was more of a feeling than anything else coming from somewhere deep inside the little dog.

"Don't hurt me. Please, don't hurt me."

Oh my. What kind of terrible road has this little one traveled to prompt such fear? The sooner we got her away from here, the better, so I pulled back on the road and continued home.

As we drove into the driveway, our other three Schnauzers came flying to the gate to welcome their new sister. I opened the truck door without thinking, and that tense bundle of dirty fur jumped up and raced down the driveway. We had a Keystone cops episode for a few minutes while I ran after her as Joey, Pip and Fitz, our threesome, raced along the inside of the fence line cheering me on.

I finally caught up with the new kid, scooped her up and went back up the drive. Once in the yard, I put her down so she could meet the other three dogs that immediately came over to say hello. There was a lot of garbled talk, and I only caught bits and pieces.

"Hey. Hi. I'm Joey. Who're you? Are you going to live here? What's your name?

"Hi. I'm Fitz. You look scared. It'll be fine. We'll take care of you."

"I'm Pip and I'm the boss here. Please keep your distance and we'll be fine."

Still no response from the new girl. She stared at all three dogs and went stumbling up the stairs toward the front door. We followed her and opened the door so she could go in the house.

Once inside, little one ran from room to room, peeing and pooping as she went. I went behind her, cleaning up, but I didn't stop her or bother her at that point. We could deal with personal habits later on. Right then I wanted her to explore and claim her territory, if that's what she needed to do.

She didn't stop for the next hour. She ran all through the house, out the sliding door, on the deck, through the yard, and then back into the house again. She was frantic. I've seen many feral cats that exhibited the same degree of panic, but I'd never met such a wild, feral dog. At first Joey thought she wanted to play. He's the official greeter, and he wants to play with any dog he sees, but finally he tuned in to her and realized that something else was going on that he couldn't fix by playing right then and there.

As our new friend raced around, I took a moment to call Animal Control and report the other dogs we'd seen, hoping that they could be taken away from that horrible house. I wasn't optimistic, but the least I could do was file a report.

While we watched the little one do warp factors around the house, we decided to call her Jenny. I don't know why; the name just seemed right. In retrospect, a year and a half later, probably Tiger would have been more appropriate, but Jenny it was.

Finally, I interrupted one of her whirlwind trips through the house to offer her some food. We'd mixed up the usual combination of dry and wet dog food with poached chicken and warm water. I stopped Jenny long enough to put the food down in front of her and watched while she devoured everything in the dish within seconds. Joey, Pip and Fitz stood by and stared in amazement as she gobbled her food. Her backbone stuck out and her ribs were clearly showing. Poor baby. I wondered when she'd last had a decent meal.

The next event had to be a bath. Even though I thought the whole ex-perience might be upsetting for our new friend, she was so filthy and smelly that I figured a bit of discomfort would be worth tolerating if a nice warm bath would make her feel better. So, I scooped her up and took her down-stairs to the laundry tub and gave her a bath. Surprisingly, she didn't mind the water at all and actually seemed to enjoy being touched. I whispered sweet nothings to her the whole time and even though she didn't respond, I felt her relax and ease into the massage that I threw in at no extra cost. After her bath, I could see that she was actually a lovely silver color. Thin, but beautiful.

So, that was our Jenny when she first arrived home.

At first, she wouldn't sleep anywhere except in the new, soft bed we bought for her, even though I put her on our bed with the other guys. She'd stay for a short time, but then she'd jump down and run to her bed. I kept moving her bed closer and closer to ours each day, and eventually she did sleep on the big bed with everyone else.

Our daily walks to the beach required some adjusting at first because we soon realized that Jenny couldn't really see or hear, and I needed to keep her on leash with me so she didn't get disoriented. After several weeks, I could let her off leash to sniff around, but I always had to stay close so she didn't feel lost. When she had those "lost" moments, she'd race back toward the truck as fast as she could, with me in pursuit.

Her health was precarious at best, but I didn't dare take her to our vet for over a month because I was sure that she'd bite him. Feral doesn't go away instantly. When I did get her in, he confirmed that her gums were still infected and she was far too thin. We'd known about the gums right away because her mouth smelled terrible, and we'd immediately started her on the antibiotics we keep on hand. The vet said that she couldn't see or hear well and that she was probably somewhere between twelve and fifteen years old. Her teeth were grungy and they needed cleaning, so I made an appointment to take care of her teeth and to give her shots the next week.

I stayed with her when she went in for her appointment because I knew that visiting a vet must be a foreign experience for her. Once her teeth and the shots were taken care of, her physical health seemed to be satisfactory, considering her age and the quality of her life before she'd come to us. That left the most important healing yet to take place.

Jenny was with us for several months before she said anything. She slept on the bed, ate well, gained weight, walked on the beach, napped during the day, went outside with the other guys to take care of personal business, rode in the truck, and generally acted like a member of the family. She developed a particular fondness for Fitz, our gentle boy who is so passive that she trusted him right away.

Watching Jenny walk along behind Fitz in the yard was such a delight. It was almost as if she were attached to him by some invisible umbilical cord. If they were cartoon characters, I knew I'd be able to see a bubble over her head that said, 'He's my brother. I like him.'

We talked to her all the time, but for months she never responded. The other dogs talked to her too, and they reassured us that she'd be fine, but they said she'd been so traumatized (my word, not theirs) that it would take her awhile to remember that she could communicate with people. Finally, she did.

One evening we all were lounging in bed watching television and Jenny was curled up next to me; I had my arm around her, as I always did. After a while, I felt her very tentatively lick my hand. She turned her head toward me and finally spoke.

"Hi."

"Well, hi yourself sweet thing. You okay?"

"Fine. Nice here. Warm. Safe."

That was the beginning. At first she only spoke in short words and her voice was hesitant and quiet. As time passed, we were able to hear her story and it became clear why she hadn't spoken right away. Apparently she'd lived her whole life with the woman who had died. Her early years were uneventful and she'd spent many long hours tied up in the backyard, although she was allowed in the house on occasion. When the woman became ill and couldn't care for her, Jenny spent most of her time curled up in her wicker basket. Sometimes people who came remembered to feed her. Sometimes they didn't.

As the woman's illness progressed, Jenny got lost in the shuffle of people coming in and out, and she retreated farther and farther into herself. After the woman died, one of her caregivers took Jenny to her home, which is where we found her. Jenny said she'd felt so alone and lost for such a long time that when we came to get her, she didn't dare hope for anyone to love her or care for her. Her story reminded me again about how important it is for people to make arrangements for the care of their animal friends in case of illness or death. Like children, animals that live with someone who is ill, must be cared for and not forgotten.

One day when we were talking, I asked her what had finally prompted her to trust us enough to speak.

"Well, I guess it was because you're all so happy here. And I feel like you care about me and want me to be part of your family. Fitz said I should trust you, and because I trust him, I decided I could talk to you."

"Fitz is right, Miss Jenny. We love you and you're a very valuable member of our family. I'm sorry about your lonely life, but you're not alone any more. Let's start from where we are now and we can all have a happy life together."

And we did. As time passed, we watched Jenny grow younger, healthier and happier every day. She filled out and her coat was shiny and soft. She loved going camping with us because she said that all of us being together twenty-four hours a day in the motor home was the perfect way for her to spend time with her family. We couldn't have agreed more. She even developed a sense of humor and took great delight in teasing Pip and playing with Joey. When she wanted to get on the bed with the rest of us, she took a flying leap and landed right where she wanted to be, even though she couldn't see where she was going. She was feisty, headstrong, demanding and much more like a Tiger than a Jenny. Not being able to see or hear didn't slow her down at all.

She loved people and joined Joey as official greeter when anyone came to the house. People who met her couldn't believe that she was a "senior citizen." She acted more like a kid. And she even started to wag her tail. It took about a year for her to feel secure and happy enough to show us this wonderful sign of contentment, but once she started, she never stopped.

One of my favorite mental pictures of Jenny is seeing her race into the house after being out in the yard. She'd come flying around the corner, tail going a mile a minute, ears (and they were big ones) flapping as she ran. Big grin. Happy dog.

Another endearing image is that of Jenny learning to eat treats from a fork or spoon. Some kind of after dinner goodie, usually some chicken or a special dog cookie, is always part of our family routine, and because the treat always involves food, Jenny would push her way to the head of the line. Even though she'd told us that she'd never eaten food from a spoon or a fork, lack of experience was quickly replaced with enthusiasm and ingenuity. Because Jenny didn't have many teeth, especially in the front, scraping food off of a spoon or fork was tricky, but she managed.

And then there was her response to the "computer-off-cookie." When I work at the computer in the afternoons, the dogs usually join me and supervise by lounging on the couch. Jenny's idea of helping was to sit on my lap while I tried to type, which was difficult at best, but I loved having her there. After I turn the computer off for the day, the dogs know that they get a treat (they say that it's in their contract); they hear the click, jump up, race into the kitchen and stand in front of the cookie bowl. Jenny couldn't hear the sound of the computer turning off, but she leaped off my lap when the other guys ran into the kitchen and stood in line with the rest of them. After a while, she became so tuned in to me that she knew when I was about to shut down for the day, and before the other dogs heard their cue, she was down on the floor, running into the kitchen so she could be first in line.

Fitz also taught her the fine art of "double dipping." He explained to her that if she sat near me at the table that I would give her a treat. Then he told her that after she'd mooched from me, she had to quickly run around to someone else sitting at the table and pretend that she hadn't had her turn. That way she'd get two goodies for the price of one smile. It worked every time.

Also, there were what she called the "beach races." Her episodes of turning and running the other direction on the beach became a real test for me. If I watched her carefully, I could tell when she was about to turn and run, and then I could put her back on leash before she did her sprint. One day I wasn't attentive enough and ended up chasing her halfway back to the parking lot.

"Okay, Miss Jenny. What's up with this business of running off?"

"Oh, Dale, it's so much fun to run and have you chase me. You taught me to play and that's what I'm doing. Lighten up. It's good exercise for you. I'm gonna run while I can. You don't need to worry about me; I won't leave the beach."

"So, you're saying that I don't need to chase you?"

"No. I want you to chase me. That's the game. You just don't need to be so serious about it. I don't feel lost anymore."

"Okay, Miss Thing. I get it. You're such a pistol. I'll play your silly game."

And so our life with Jenny continued for another year and a half before it was time for her to leave us. But she never really left- not in the most important sense. When we walk on the beach we know she's there. We can see her bouncing along ahead of us, turning every once in a while to give us that impish grin and an enthusiastic wag of her tail. I can almost hear her saying, "Catch me if you can!" Joey, Pip and Fitz feel her too because we can see them stop and wait to be sure she's with us.

She's always with us. For a small dog, she was a considerable presence while she was here and that presence continues to be felt by all of us. Selfishly, we wish that she was still with us in body, but we're so grateful that she was able to stay as long as she did. At night I still feel her snugged up next to me. I dream about her and with her all the time. I can see her now in the rear garden as I write these words. Her wonderful voice that got stronger and stronger the more she was loved, still rings in my ears. Not a whisper … a strong, healthy voice.

"Hey, my family! I love you all. I'll send someone else. You wait and see."

And she did. Five months after Jenny left us, Angus joined our family. Interestingly enough, he came to us on the same date that Jenny arrived two years earlier, March 22.

But that's another story ...

An Afternoon at the Beach

The American Staffordshire Terrier that caught the Frisbee was an amazing athlete. At first, I didn't think she was running fast enough, but she anticipated the throw even before it happened. Seconds before the disc was actually launched, the dog was already running, feet furiously churning up sand. Her timing was perfect.

The red saucer looked out of reach, but in a perfectly balanced move, the dog leaped up, grabbed it, and ran back to her person. She dropped the Frisbee at the feet of the guy who'd thrown it and sat there grinning from ear to ear. "More! Throw it again! C'mon. Let's go!"

"Okay, Sadie, go for it!" And off she went again. Another great catch.

Sadie. What an incongruous name for such a beautiful athlete. Her lovely brindle colored coat gleamed and her white chest fur looked like a tuxedo shirt. A very classy look for a classy lady. She was having such a good time. It was obvious that this game was one that she and her friend played often. There was lots of hugging and carrying on each time the Frisbee was returned. It was hard to tell who was having more fun, the dog or the man. Together they made a great team. As I watched them, I found myself wishing that people who have such a negative bias about this breed, (more commonly called Pit Bull), could see this magnificent dog and her friend playing together. I also thought about those people who train dogs of Sadie's breed to fight, and wished that each and every one of them could be chained to a post and be eaten by ants. My level of tolerance for such inhumane activities is minus-zero.

Having negative thoughts in such a wonderful place was counter-productive, so I shifted my focus and looked around at the dogs and humans who had come to play at this beach park. This section of the beach is one of several designated parks on the island where people can come with their dogs and enjoy the beach without having to use leashes. The beach is maintained by volunteers who are members of FETCH. (Free Exercise Time for Canines and their Humans), a local organization dedicated to creating and maintaining areas like this one. There wasn't a scrap of paper or trash anywhere, and there were "doggie-waste-bags" available for the necessary clean-up chores.

I'd recently heard about the park and was checking it out for the first time to see if it was a place our dog friends would enjoy. So far what I'd seen was encouraging and certainly warranted a return visit with our Schnauzers.

"So, ya know what he did then? He knows I like to be outside a lot, but he worries about my being out in the rain or the hot sun, so he rigged up this big ole beach umbrella and he put it up under a tree so I could lie on my blanket and not get wet or too hot. Isn't that somethin'?"

The dog telling the story was a big Malamute with a heavy coat. She was walking with a Beagle, which in itself was a charming sight. They stopped near me and I continued to eavesdrop on their conversation.

"Well, yeah, Nakita, that's great. You've got a terrific human there. Is that him over there under that big striped umbrella?"

"Yep, that's him. When we come to the beach, like today, he brings the umbrella for himself and then when I feel like it, I can lie under it too. He's a thoughtful guy. What's your person like, Barney?"

"Terrific. I get to go everywhere my people go, unless they go on an airplane trip, and then I get to stay with friends. I like being inside and my favorite place to sleep is on the back of the sofa. If I sleep up there I don't miss anything. It's neat."

As the two dogs moved out of my hearing range, I watched them until a big floppy Bearded Collie barreled over to me and plopped himself down in front of me.

"Hi! I'm Higgins. Is your name Dale?"

"Hi, Higgins, yes, I'm Dale. What's up?"

"Oh, nuthin'. I'm hanging out with my friend. She's the pretty lady over there talking to that guy with the Frisbee. Got any candy?"

"Candy? Dogs can't eat candy; you'll get sick."

"Yeah, but I really really love chocolate. I get into trouble at home all the time because I can find chocolate anywhere. I love it! Got any?"

"No, Higgins, sorry I don't. How about a dog cookie?"

"Well, okay, if that's all you've got. Wish it was chocolate, though."

I gave Higgins a cookie from the supply I always keep in my pocket and it disappeared in seconds. He gave me a quick grin of thanks before he bounded away toward his friend. She saw him coming and bent down, arms wide, welcoming him back. She kissed him, rubbed his ears, whispered something that I couldn't hear, and he ran off again in search of who knows what. His ears flopped as he ran. Sadie saw him running, dropped the Frisbee, and soon the two of them were racing down the beach. Higgins couldn't keep up but he gave it his best shot. Finally he stopped and shook his head.

Sadie turned long enough to see that Higgins wasn't following her and came back to sit next to him. I couldn't hear what they were saying, but they had their heads together. Pretty soon Nakita and Barney joined them, and it looked like some kind of football huddle. I wondered what kind of play they were planning.

My attention was diverted from the huddle by two white streaks that flashed by me. Two beautiful white Shepherds were playing tag. They'd both obviously been in the water because they were wet and sandy, but were they having fun!

"C'mon, Snowball! Catch me if you can!"

"Hey, Enoki, I'm all over it. I've gotcha!"

With a flurry of sand and wet fur, both dogs raced in circles around me and Snowball took a flying leap and landed on top of Enoki. Both of them went down, feet flying. They landed in a heap right in front of me, and I ended up covered with sand and water too.

"Hi guys, having fun?"

Both dogs stopped playing to look up at me long enough to give me big happy grins.

"Ooops, sorry. We didn't mean to get you dirty. It's all Enoki's fault. He's always running in the water and then I have to catch him. Happens all the time. I always get him, though. He's not fast enough for me."

"Yeah, sure. You don't always catch me and you know it. Remember the other day? You ate my dust!"

Just like a couple of kids. I reached over, brushed sand from their noses, and said that I didn't mind a little water and sand. No point in coming to the beach if I want to stay clean. I told them how beautiful they were and while they were resting up for their next round, I wandered down the beach a little farther.

There was a volleyball game in progress. Somebody had rigged up a makeshift net by tying a rope between two tall sticks that were jammed in the sand. The players did have a real volleyball though and it looked like it had seen action in many games. There were two people on each side of the "net" and they were good, but the star of the game was an Australian Cattle Dog. I figured that she'd catch the ball with her teeth and run off with it. Wrong. This dog was a player.

As I watched in amazement, I saw her bump the ball with her nose toward her human partner. The young woman had to dive to get the ball, but she managed to scoop it up and send it over the net.

"Way to go, Pearl! Nice hit!

Pearl raced around, keeping track of the ball and every time it came near her, she bumped it toward the person closest to her. She was so fast! At first I thought the team that had Pearl on their side had an unfair advantage, but she didn't play favorites. Actually, she played both sides of the net and helped to score points for both teams. A very fair dog.

The amazing thing about Pearl was that she didn't have the use of her rear legs, at least not in a traditional sense. She was strapped in a cart that had two wheels, which served as her back legs. Her own apparently useless rear legs dangled from the cart. Incredible. She moved around in that cart like a true athlete. I wonder if there's a Special Olympics for dogs?

I wanted to talk to Pearl and hear her story, but I didn't want to interrupt the game. Maybe I could see her later. I smiled to myself and wondered what the game would be like if only dogs were playing. The rope might have to be lowered a bit, but I was sure they could manage. I could see Sadie and Pearl playing against Enoki and Snowball. What a game that would be! Wonderful stuff.

I watched the volleyball action for a while and then continued down the beach. I clearly was out of place here without a dog. I'd have to come back with our gang of four. Joey would love it. I could see him as the official greeter. Another day.

"Molly! Lilly! Get back here! Leave Jake alone!"

Two little Bichon Frises were chasing a big lumbering chocolate Lab down the beach. The human who belonged to them was running after all of them. They headed straight for me and before I had a chance to move out of the way, the Lab ran up and hid behind me.

"Hey, lady, you gotta save me. Those maniacs are after me again. I don't wanna run anymore."

This must be Jake. And the two maniacs were now right in front of me, dancing around, trying to get Jake to run again.

"C'mon Jake, you know you need the exercise. Get moving!"

"Hey, guys, what's going on?"

They all started talking at once, and I couldn't understand what any of them were saying. Finally the human joined the group, scooped up the two small dogs and held one in each arm. Their feet were still pumping at high speed, even though they weren't going anywhere. The man smiled at me and explained that Jake was overweight and the two Bichons had taken it upon themselves to give him some exercise by chasing him. The only problem was that they weren't ready to quit when Jake was tired. They fancied themselves as his personal trainers and felt it necessary to push him. No pain, no gain was their philosophy. Jake sat behind me, grinning sheepishly.

I laughed and asked Jake why he bothered to run away from them.

"Aw, they'd hate it if I didn't run. I like the girls and I guess I do need the exercise. But, they're so darn perky. They don't know when to quit."

The man put the girls down and they immediately bounded over to Jake, climbed all over him, licked him and pulled his hair. He sat there patiently enduring their antics, well loved by his dog sisters and his human. Perfect. What a great family.

I thanked Jake, Molly, Lilly and their human friend for the visit and continued to walk toward the water, but I hadn't taken more than a few steps before I heard a shout.

"Surf's up, dude! Let's catch a wave!"

Surf's up? Here? Not hardly. This wasn't California or Hawaii. I'd never seen anyone surfing on this island. Oh, maybe wind surfing on a blustery, wintry day off the west side, but regular surfing? I don't think so.

The two dogs that were racing out to catch the wave didn't know there wasn't any surfing going on here. They didn't have any boards, although with what I'd already seen today, I wouldn't have been surprised if they did have surfboards. What I saw were two Golden Retrievers, racing neck and neck to catch a wave.

"C'mon, Tank. Hustle your buns. We're gonna miss this wave."

"No, we're not, Jake. Here it comes. Go for it!"

Both dogs threw themselves flat at the incoming wave and were lifted up by the water. Now, we're not talking giant waves here, but there was enough of a lift to give them both a ride back to shore.

As I watched them, I moved closer to the water, I guess because I wanted to be sure they were all right. I needn't have worried. Not only were they all right, but they were up and racing back out to catch the next wave before I could even say their names.

Another Jake and his friend Tank. A couple of island surfer dudes. Indeed.

"Aren't they something?" "Those guys are too much." The two women who'd come to stand next to me watched the dogs with what could only be interpreted as looks of pure love and pride on their faces. "They love the water." "Look at 'em go!"

"How did they learn to do that?" I was amazed at their enthusiasm and athleticism.

"Oh, I'm not sure exactly." One of the women answered my question. "I've been taking Jake to the beach ever since he was a puppy, and one day we met my friend here and Tank. Both dogs sort of got into the habit of chasing the waves. Eventually they figured out that it was more fun to ride them than chase them. They do this all the time. We always watch closely to be sure they don't tackle something they can't handle, but they seem to know what to do. For a couple of roughnecks, they're pretty careful."

Well, the roughnecks were certainly having a wonderful time. I watched awhile longer, thinking that I probably should be going soon, but this was the best show in town and I was having such a good time I was reluctant to leave. Maybe I could stay a few more minutes.

I hadn't even moved before I heard more voices, this time coming from a pair of dogs that were walking toward me.

"Honest to God, Satch. You're dumber than a sack of rocks. How could you not know you were sitting on her?"

"Well, gee, Uki, I dunno. I heard this kitty crying and couldn't figure out where the noise was coming from. I didn't know I was sitting on her. I didn't mean it. I didn't hurt her, honest!"

Satch was a big English Sheepdog and Uki was a multi-colored Lab mix of some sort. Uki was giving Satch a bad time about something he'd done that she clearly thought was dumb. I was too curious to keep walking, so I stopped and asked what they were talking about. Nice thing about dogs is that they don't ever think humans are rude when they interrupt conversations.

They both stopped and Uki explained that the other day Satch sat on one of the foster kitties that lives at their house and when the kitten squealed, he couldn't figure out where the noise was coming from. Uki thought he was dumb for doing such a thing. She thought he should have known better.

"So, I guess you guys must live together?"

"Yeah, there's the two of us, and Kira and Bambi. They're both dog sisters. Bambi's shy. And, we got a new girl the other day - a puppy that was at the shelter and has a broken leg. Her name's Katie. She's not gonna live with us forever, but only 'til her leg gets better. Nolan used to be with us too, but he died and I got to come and live there after that. We have lots of cats and kittens that live with us too. Our human takes care of baby kittens until they're old enough to be adopted. Satch sat on one of the kittens."

"I told you, Uki, I couldn't help it. Those kittens are always all over everything. How was I supposed to know that one had crawled under me when I was sleeping? I was taking a nap, minding my own business."

"I know, I know, but, you gotta be more careful. They're little guys and you know they like to crawl up into your fur because you're so warm."

I had the feeling that this was an ongoing banter between these two friends. Uki was being Lucy to Satch's Charlie Brown. I knew she liked him in spite of her nagging because when he looked kind of dejected about the bad time she was giving him, she moved closer and gave him a big slurp.

"I know you didn't mean it, ya big lug. You're too sweet to hurt anything. C'mon, let's find Doreen and the girls. Maybe she's looking for us."

"Nice to meet you two." I called after them as they ran off, but I don't think they heard me.

I was about to turn back, but my attention was caught by a large black Rottweiler headed toward me. The beautiful dog was pulling a red cart, and in the cart were two puppies. What did we have here? Looked like the dog version of Mom taking the babies for a walk in a stroller. A slim, gray haired woman walked next to the cart, her hand lightly resting on the big dog's back.

As they approached me, I went over to them, introduced myself to the woman, and asked about the dog and the cart.

The woman smiled and answered my question. "This is Princess. The puppies needed some fresh air and socializing, Princess loves pulling the cart, so here we are. If we walk on the packed sand it's no harder for her than walking on a sidewalk or a street. And, it's so lovely here. We come several times a week."

Princess gave me a great smile and held out her paw. I smiled back as I took her paw and gently rubbed her soft fur. The woman went on to explain about Princess and the cart. "She likes to work; we often walk in parades and she loves it. She's very gentle and careful."

Princess stood patiently while we were talking, but once the cart had stopped, the sleeping puppies woke up and started squirming around, trying to get out of the cart.

"Hi little ones. Is Princess your mom?"

They both started talking at the same time. "Oh, no. Wish she were though. She's so big and soft." "We don't have a mom yet, but the nice lady here is taking care of us 'til we're old enough to be 'dopted. Wanna 'dopt us?"

By now, I couldn't resist and was holding both soft furry bodies as I responded. I just love puppy breath. "I'd love to adopt you both, but I already have four dog friends at home. I'm sure someone wonderful will come along and adopt you when you're ready. In the meantime, you get to live with Princess and her friend. Pretty neat deal."

"Actually, it's wonderful," the woman responded, as she ran her hand over Princess's shiny black coat. It was clear that these two had a quite a loving relationship. "These pups were abandoned at the shelter and I'm fostering them until they're old enough to be adopted. There were actually six in the litter, but one of them died, and the other three are with another foster family. Princess is incredibly good with them, and I love having puppies in the house."

"Isn't it hard to give the puppies up when it's time for them to return to the shelter?"

"Oh, yes it is; but we screen people carefully, and we'll find the right family for them."

"And they will too." Princess lifted her paw to get my attention. " This lady's my mom-friend. I was at the shelter too. I made such a fuss and noise whenever she walked by my cage, she finally gave in and took me home with her. I guess I was kinda hard to adopt because I'm so big. My friend couldn't resist me though, and now I have a great home and we love each other."

"Well, I can certainly see that you would be hard to resist, Princess. You're so beautiful. It's been a pleasure to meet all of you. I won't keep you from your walk. Let me put the little guys back in the cart and you can be on your way."

I reluctantly settled the puppies back in the cart and off they went. When the cart started to move, the puppies quieted back down. As they walked down the beach, I thought about the many ways humans feel love and kindness toward their animal friends, and how those feelings manifest themselves in so many wonderful ways.

I really did have to go, so I turned and headed back down the beach. Uki and Satch had found the rest of their family, and I saw them racing around with two black dogs and a young Golden Retriever that was limping, while the woman with them was collecting rocks. The Retrievers, Tank and Jake, were still riding the waves. Molly, Lilly and Jake the Lab were flaked out on the sand, the two girls asleep on Jake's back. Pearl was continuing to hold her own in the volleyball game. Enoki and Snowball were now walking quite sedately with their humans. Higgins and his lady were sitting with their backs resting against a piece of driftwood. Higgins was staring intently at something the lady was eating; I'm sure he was hoping it was chocolate. Nakita and Barney were still deep in conversation. Sadie was lying down, the Frisbee clutched between her two front paws. She looked tired, but she wasn't about to give up her prize.

When I arrived at my car, I sat there for a minute thinking about all that I'd seen and I knew I'd be back. I wondered if my friend Pip would chase the Frisbee with Sadie, or whether she'd try to eat it. There's only one way to find out. Tomorrow I'll bring the Schnauzer gang and we'll really have some fun.

Casper

"Soooooo c-c-c-c-old. Someb-b-b-b-ody, please h-h-h-elp."

I'd been taking a nap and I sat straight up. What was I hearing? Who was cold? Who needed help? Certainly couldn't be our four Schnauzers who were out running errands with Ellaine. No one else was home.

Without even knowing where I was going, I put on my warm jacket and went outside. It was freezing! The temperature had dropped to a record low of nine degrees; snow and ice covered the ground. I stood in the front yard, listening. The air was so still I could hear myself breathing, but I couldn't hear anything else. I started walking, hoping I'd find whoever was in trouble.

As I crossed the street, I looked toward the house at the end of the cul-de-sac, but I knew that no one was home. I'd seen the family who lived there leave earlier in the day, the car packed with suitcases and presents. They had moved in a couple of weeks ago and were probably going away for the Christmas holidays. But, something drew me toward their house. And then, I heard it again.

"Please ... soooo c-c-c-cold."

The sound was coming from the back yard of the house where no one was home. I walked faster, slipping and sliding on the ice and snow. When I finally made it to the back of the house I could hardly believe what I was seeing.

There was a dog in a pen that was enclosed with chain link fencing. A cage. (I know that people call them kennels, but no matter how you cut it, kennels are cages.) He was lying on top of a dog house that had been placed inside the pen, and he was shaking so badly that the dog house actually moved under his shivering body. The concrete floor of the cage was covered with feces. What little water there was in a dirty bowl was frozen solid. Another empty bowl was upended in the corner. I could see inside the dog house and what I saw made my skin crawl. On the floor was a dirty wet cotton blanket, covered with maggots. No wonder he was on top of the dog house!

As soon as he saw me coming toward him, the dog jumped down and stumbled over to the gate of the cage. His teeth were chattering so much I could hardly understand him.

"Th th th th anks for cccoming … ssso cccold."

I opened the gate and he literally fell into my arms, knocking me to the ground. I knew that I had to get him warm, so I stood up and encouraged him to follow me. He tried to walk, but he could hardly stand. I picked him up and rushed back to my house with his shivering body draped over my shoulder. Fortunately I didn't have far to go because carrying a full size Spaniel on ice and snow wasn't a graceful dance, but we made it. We staggered in through the downstairs door because it was easier than trying to carry him up the stairs to the front door. As soon as we got inside, I laid him down while I grabbed blankets, wrapped him up, and held him as close to me as I could. Both of us were shaking because he was so cold his body vibrated.

Finally, I could feel my body heat begin to warm him and his shaking began to subside. He was painfully thin and his coat was matted and wet. I felt like I wanted to give him a warm bath right away, but first I needed some answers.

"All right, my friend. What's going on? Who are you and why were you outside in the cold?"

"Casper … live there. People went away. Sorry bothered you. Thanks for hearing. So cold."

"Casper, I'm Dale, and you didn't bother me at all. I'm glad I was able to hear you. I didn't even know you were there. How could your people leave you outside in this weather?"

"Outside all the time."

"But, they just went away and left you? How could they do that? What's wrong with them?"

"Leave all the time. Others feed sometimes. Not enough food. So cold."

By now, he'd warmed up enough so I could sit back and look at him. A closer look revealed that not only was he terribly thin, wet and matted, but the bottoms of his feet were raw and bleeding. His coat was dull and what I assumed to be brown and white fur was covered with slime and dirt. He had a cute topknot of hair that stuck straight up, big brown eyes, a great smile and beautiful teeth. He must be young-a baby.

"How old are you, Casper?"

"Dunno … don't know about age. Feel sorta young. You?"

"I'm sixty-five, but I think I'm in better shape than you are."

"Yeah, maybe. Look pretty bad, huh?"

"Well, let's say that the first thing we need to do is get you cleaned up. I want to get rid of these mats and tangles before I bathe you though, or they'll shrink up and bother you even more."

I grabbed a pair of scissors and got to work. Casper liked being fussed over and he relaxed while I cut the mats and cleaned the bottoms of his feet with warm water. Then, I took him upstairs and after I took my clothes off, we both got into the shower. Taking a shower with a dog is messy business, but he was so dirty that I thought the shower would be better than a bath. He loved the warm water and even though he tried to shake himself dry every time I turned the water off to shampoo some more, it was a pretty successful shower. For both of us.

Finally he was clean and I asked him to stay put while I got dressed. I found more towels and dried him as best I could before we went into the living room to light a fire.

Once the fire was going, I wrapped him in another blanket and asked him to stay in front of the fire and get warm.

"No problem. Not going anywhere. Nice. Thanks. Hey, other dogs live here. Where? Outside?"

"Outside? No way. They went for a ride to the store with Ellaine."

"A ride? Neat. Never get to go for rides. Do they like it?"

"Yeah, they love it. But never mind them right now. Are you hungry? Would you like some food?"

"Oh, yeah. Hungry."

Mumbling to myself about insensitive people who leave their dogs outside to freeze, I went into the kitchen to fix him something to eat. I mixed canned food, dry food, cooked chicken and warm water together in a big bowl, which I brought into the living room. He was sound asleep in front of the fire. I knew he was hungry, but he was probably exhausted too, so I set the bowl down and figured that he needed to sleep right then. Food could come later.

After I made myself a cup of coffee, I went in to sit near him. I was furious! Here was a wonderful animal that wasn't being cared for, on any level. Poor guy was caged, lonely, cold and hungry. Why do people bother to invite animals into their lives if they aren't going to welcome them as members of the family? What's the point? Where's the common sense? How in the world could it possibly be acceptable to keep an animal outside in extreme cold? Sure, there are heavy coated dogs that love being outside in winter, but they have the bulk and thick coats to accommodate the weather. This was a skinny dog with feathery fur that wouldn't keep him warm at all, and he was living in filth.

I could tell that he'd been caged a long time because his communication skills were limited. That's what being in a cage does to an animal. When a dog's world doesn't extend beyond a cage, his intuitive sense of the world is very limited. Confined. All of that wonderful intuition is trapped.

Caged animals don't communicate well because they can't "see" beyond the confines of the cage. When we talked he never referred to himself using "I" or any other personal pronoun. This was a dog that had no sense of his own identity at all because his people had depressed this important need by caging him.

While I ranted and raved to myself, I began to think about what to do with Casper. Without a doubt I needed to get him away from the people who were neglecting him, but how to do that was a problem. We were relatively new to the island too and I didn't know anyone who could take him. I couldn't keep him here because I knew that the people would come home eventually and sooner or later they'd know he was at our house. They might go door to door looking for him, and I could hardly keep him hidden. As it was, I was already guilty of trespassing and dog napping.

So what. I never thought twice about getting him out of there, and I wasn't about to worry about legalities now.

"Hey, food?"

"Hi, buddy. Yeah, this is for you. I didn't want to wake you, but help yourself."

In a matter of seconds the bowl was clean and Casper was looking for more. As much as I wanted to keep feeding him, I knew that he needed to eat often rather than huge amounts at one time. He was so thin I knew his stomach wouldn't be able to handle large portions.

"Not to worry, Casper. You can have more later. It isn't good for you to eat too much at one time."

"Okay. Good stuff. What was it?"

I told him what was in his meal, brought him some water, and after he'd had a drink, he curled up beside me. The warmth of the fire was drying his coat nicely, and now I could see his beautiful brown and white colors. His coat was soft and he smelled good.

"So, my friend. What am I going to do with you?"

"Dunno. You figure it out. Need to sleep. S'nice here." And with that, he was asleep again. He'd used up all of his energy trying to stay warm, and hadn't even come close to succeeding at that.

While Casper slept, I made a few calls, trying to find someone who would be willing to keep him or help find him a home. I knew that taking him away wasn't legal, but I figured that anyone who would neglect a dog to this extent didn't deserve to have him. He needed to live inside with people who loved him. The people who kept him in the pen probably wouldn't even miss him. The recipients of my calls were all sympathetic, but no one was willing to take him. Finally, after several calls, someone suggested that I call the animal shelter. The person who recommended the shelter said that she thought it was a pretty nice place and that they'd take care of him. She also said that she knew the inside part of the area where dogs were kept was heated at night during the winter if the temperature dropped below thirty degrees.

Given what I know now, I wouldn't have called the shelter. I would have figured out something else. But, I was naïve and thought that rescuing Casper was simply a matter of doing the right thing. I imagined the shelter as a place where he could be safe, warm, and he'd be taken away from the people who had neglected him. If he were a child, protective services would have him out of that house in a heartbeat.

The person at the shelter who took my call was horrified by what I told her about Casper's physical condition and his living quarters, but she didn't like my having removed him from the premises. She suggested that perhaps I could create some warmth in his dog house with clean blankets and leave him there until his people came home. I told her that I understood her concerns, and was aware of the fact that I had broken the law by taking him to my house without permission, but there was no way that I was willing to leave him outside in the cold. Then she asked if I could I keep him at my house until his people returned. I was reluctant to tell her that I didn't want the people to know his whereabouts, so we discussed the situation for a while and it soon became clear to her that I simply wasn't going to put the dog back outside. I was about ready to hang up when she finally said that they'd take him if I agreed to tell his people where he was as soon as they returned home.

Talk about being between and rock and a hard place. I didn't want those uncaring, insensitive people to know where he was. I wanted the shelter to magically find a home for him before his people returned from their trip. I wanted a happy ending. After telling the woman at the shelter that I'd think about her offer and call her back, I hung up.

Casper was still sleeping, so I left him in front of the fire and walked over to his house to take a closer look at his prison. I don't know what I was thinking. Maybe I was hoping that I'd overreacted and I could clean things up and make a warm place for him. I don't know. But, when I took a closer look, what I saw was even worse than what I'd seen on my initial visit. It was also clear that the cage hadn't gotten in this condition over night. No attempt had been made to keep the cage clean. Not today. Not yesterday. Not ever. I knew the people had only lived here for a couple of weeks, so I suppose what I saw was two week's worth of poop. Both food and water dishes were so dirty that it was hard to imagine any living creature being asked to take nourishment from them. I pulled the blanket out of the dog house and not only was it wet; it was soggy. It had obviously been that way for quite some time. As I laid the blanket out on the cement, maggots squirmed all over. Maggots don't breed in just a day or two in freezing weather.

I stormed back to our house, even more convinced that I couldn't leave Casper in that mess. He was still asleep by the fire. I sat down next to him and ran my hands over his boney back. I didn't want to wake him, but I did need to talk with him.

"Hey, Casper. Could we talk for a minute?"

He yawned, stretched and flopped a paw on my knee. "Sure. What's up? More food?"

"Not yet, my friend. In a while. I need to talk with you about what to do with you. I need your opinion."

"Okay. Whaddaya want to know?"

"Well, I know that I'm not going to put you back in that cage. I also know that I don't want those people to have you. They aren't taking care of you and you deserve much better. The woman at the animal shelter said that you can come there, but if you do, she said I have to tell your people where you are when they come home. I don't want them to know where you are; that's why you can't stay here. What I need to know from you is what you want me to do."

"Well, uh … is the, what you call it, animal shelter, a nice place?"

"I don't know, Casper. I've been told that it is, but I haven't been there. The woman who talked to me on the phone was very nice and really sympathetic."

"Other dogs there? Like other dogs. Miss brothers and sisters."

"Yeah, I'm sure there are lots of other dogs there. That's why it's called an animal shelter."

"Food there? Warm?"

"I'm sure they have food, and I was told that they turn the heat on at night in the winter. I don't know what it would be like during the day."

"Not so bad. Not as nice as here. Hide me here?"

"I don't think that would work. You'd have to go outside sooner or later and they'd see you."

"Yeah, okay, let's go. See the other dogs."

"All right, but I'm worried about what will happen when your people come home. If I take you to the shelter, I have to agree to tell your people where you are when they come home. What if they go to the shelter to get you and bring you back to your horrible cage? I don't want that to happen."

"Maybe won't come. Never pay any attention. Maybe won't matter if not there. Trust you. Don't worry."

As I listened to him, I really wanted to believe that what he said was true. And, the more I thought about it, the more I became convinced that the people might not even bother to bail him out of the shelter. Why would they? If they were willing to leave him out in the cold, then why would they care where he was? Maybe they needed an excuse to give him away. I just was worried because Casper trusted me to do the right thing and I couldn't let him down.

Even though I heard a small warning voice inside my head, I caved in and called the woman at the shelter. She gave me directions and I told her we'd be there soon.

I fed Casper once more and left a note for Ellaine telling her where I'd gone. Then I bagged up all of Casper's mats and tangles so the people at the shelter could see what a mess he'd been, and we hopped in the truck. It wasn't a long ride to the shelter, but he loved every minute of it. He sat up straight in the passenger seat and didn't miss a thing. What a great dog!

The shelter wasn't open to the public when we arrived, but the woman on the phone had explained to me how I could drive around the side and come in the back door. I grabbed the leash I always keep in the truck, hooked Casper up and we went inside the shelter. He was so excited that he squirmed every which way as he lapped up all the attention he received from the people in the office. They told him how handsome he was and that he was welcome there. He was more interested in finding out where the other dogs were, but he was polite and enjoyed the attention. I was impressed with the greeting he received and was eager to go through my story once again after it was explained to me that my report would be given to the animal control officer. I gave a detailed accounting of Casper's living situation, and the condition he'd been in when I found him.

The more I talked, the more I became convinced that this would be fine. Everyone in the office thought that he was a great candidate for adoption, and in fact they said there were several people on a waiting list who were looking for a Springer Spaniel. They told me that they screened their applicants thoroughly and showed me a copy of the adoption profile they had people fill out when they came to adopt a dog. They said that he'd be available for adoption as soon as his people officially "surrendered" him, or if they didn't show up to claim him, he'd be available five days after they'd been notified that he was there. I reassured them that I'd tell his people where he was as soon as they returned home.

I asked if I could check out the premises and left Casper in the office while I went outside. Cages are cages, no matter where they are, but the cages were clean and each had an inside area that could be kept warm at night by closing a doggie door. I'd been reassured that the heat was turned on at night, and so I knew that Casper would at least be warm at night. On the floor in the inside part of each cage was a sleeping platform with a blanket; food and water bowls hung on the lower portion of the inside of each cage.

The place was a madhouse! There were thirty-two cages, all except two filled with barking dogs. As I walked down the outside aisle I saw dogs of every imaginable shape and size. Most of them were big. All of them were noisy. It was like a college dormitory run amok. But, the dogs all looked fine, and at least they were safe. I hated seeing the dogs in cages, but I balanced that uneasiness with the truth that for some of them, (Casper included) this was probably better than wherever they'd been before they were brought to the shelter.

I went back into the office to find Casper sprawled on the floor getting his stomach rubbed by one of the staff people. I kneeled down in front of him and said, "I think it's gonna be fine, Casper. There are lots and lots of dogs out there."

He jumped up and headed for the door. He was ready. I explained to the staff that Casper liked other dogs and was anxious to meet them. They said that he'd have his own kennel (their word, not mine), but he'd be surrounded by dogs and there was an exercise pen outside where he could play with other dogs the next day. A shy and frightened dog had come in the day before and they thought that maybe Casper's outgoing nature would help her to relax, so they were going to put him in a kennel opposite her.

After reassuring the staff that I'd contact his people as soon as they returned home, I gave Casper a final hug and told him I'd see him soon. I got a quick slurp in return, but he was clearly anxious to get out there and check out the other dogs. I felt like he was in good hands when I left the shelter and returned to our house.

I visited Casper at the shelter for the next couple of days. Everyone loved him and apparently there were several people who had come in and were interested in adopting him. He barked and carried on with the other dogs, and he seemed to be doing fine. He said he didn't mind the noise at all because it was a change from being alone all the time. It was cold there during the day, but at least he could go into the inside portion of his cage and stay relatively warm because he had a nice warm blanket on his sleeping platform. The doggie door between the inside and the outside portions of his cage stayed open during the day so he could come and go. As a courtesy, I was allowed to take him for walks when I went to see him even though I wasn't officially a volunteer. I didn't see anyone walking the other dogs and asked whether they ever got out.

It was explained to me that there were volunteers who came to walk the dogs, but there weren't many of them and the dogs didn't always get out every day. I thought that maybe I could help and promised to start coming in to volunteer on a regular basis. Shelter staff were doing everything they could to help the dogs (and many cats that were there), but they needed more volunteers.

On the evening of the third day of Casper's stay at the shelter, his people came home. It was late when I heard their car go past our house, but since I didn't feel like getting out of bed to go down and talk to them, I decided to wait until the next morning. Okay, I was stalling. I was awake most of the night, anticipating a knock on the door and planning what I would say to them. I knew that I couldn't be angry and say what I really wanted to say because I didn't want them to be defensive. I kept telling myself that I had to be calm and reasonable if I was going to convince them to leave Casper at the shelter. I went over and over what I would say, and finally it was morning and there was no putting it off any longer.

I'll admit that I was dragging my feet as I walked across the street, but I'd promised and I believe in keeping my promises. When a man answered the door, I introduced myself and asked if I could come in and talk with him about Casper. In my most reasonable, calm, non-accusatory tone, I explained where Casper was, how he had gotten there, and that he was fine. I talked about what a great dog he was and how much I liked him. I went on to say that there were several people who were interested in adopting him if they'd be willing to leave him at the shelter. I felt like I talked for hours, but I know my monologue couldn't have lasted that long.

The man never said anything the whole time I talked. I wanted to ask him questions, but I knew that I probably wouldn't like any of the answers, so I ended up repeating myself and telling him that the shelter would be happy to find a home for Casper. Eventually I ran out of words, because short of telling him what a jerk I thought he was there wasn't anything else to say. Finally, I stopped talking, hoping for some kind of response. All he did was thank me for coming as he showed me the door.

That was it. No questions. No explanations. Just, "Thank you for coming." The only response that might have made the encounter even more absurd than it was would have been his telling me to have a nice day. As I walked back home I thought that maybe he was embarrassed and didn't know what to say. If that was the case, I had no sympathy at all. He should have felt more than embarrassment for keeping an animal in such deplorable conditions. Well, it wouldn't do any good to try to second guess what he was thinking. I'd said my piece and now it was a matter of waiting to see what would happen.

When I returned home, I called the shelter and told them that Casper's people were back, and that I had told them he was at the shelter. I asked if there had been any calls left on their answering machine last night or this morning to report him as a lost dog, and they said that no one had called. That was a good sign; maybe they didn't want him. When I asked what would happen next, the staff person said that Casper's five day waiting period would now officially begin since his people had been notified as to his whereabouts. She also said that my report had been given to the animal control officer and he would take it from there. She added that they all thought Casper was a wonderful dog and they hoped he'd be available for adoption because many people were interested in him.

There didn't seem to be anything else I could do, so I spent the day running errands and trying to keep busy. What I really wanted to do was to go to the shelter and station myself inside of Casper's cage. I wanted to make sure that he stayed right where he was. But, I did the adult thing and went about my business. Avoidance? Denial? Who knows? I thought about going to the shelter to see Casper, but I figured that maybe I'd better stay away, at least for this day.

Late in the afternoon after I'd returned from doing my meaningless errands, I received a call from the animal control officer. He told me that he had read my report, but he insisted that I go through all of the information again. He wanted to know if I'd taken pictures of the pen and the blanket.

Pictures? I told him that I hadn't even thought about taking pictures. I was more concerned about getting the dog out of there. He said that even though he thought my concern was admirable, I had broken the law by removing the dog from the premises without permission. He also said that he was sorry I hadn't taken photographs because they would visually support my claim of neglect. The more he talked, the more I began to get a very bad feeling. Finally I interrupted him and asked the only question that was important to me at the moment.

"So, where is Casper right now?"

"The family who owns him came to get him earlier this afternoon. He's back at home with them."

I'm not often speechless, but I was at that moment. My worst fear had been realized. Casper trusted me and I let him down.

"Do you mean to tell me that after all the information you were given about the neglect of this animal, you let the people who neglected him take him home? How could you do that? Doesn't he have any rights?"

"Sure, he has rights, but these people just need some education about how to care for him. They promised that they'd do better, and I'm going out to their house tomorrow to see what I can do to help them."

"Education? Look, officer, I've been a teacher for many years, and I know that there are some things that are definitely NOT a matter of education. This is one of them. These people don't have the mentality to be educated on this issue. They obviously have no common sense and they certainly have no compassion. No amount of education can instill compassion in people with regard to the care of animals. You're kidding yourself if you think that talking to them is going to make any difference at all. They aren't the ones who need help."

"I'm sorry you feel that way, but there isn't enough evidence of neglect to warrant impounding the animal, which I would love to do, believe me. He isn't injured in any way. You're the only one who's broken the law. I'll talk to them, but that's all I can do right now. Your complaint has been filed."

"Why would they want him back? You saw the bag of mats and tangles I removed from his coat. They obviously can't be bothered to take care of him. You read my report about the condition of the cage. Did you even look at the dog? Did you see how skinny he is?"

"Yes, I saw him. He's thin, but I've seen worse. He'll gain some weight once they have him neutered. And, as far as why they wanted him back, I didn't talk to them, but I'll be seeing them tomorrow. And, quite frankly, it's none of your business. He isn't your dog. They own him and they have a right to keep him if they want him. After all, he's a purebred Springer Spaniel that's worth a lot of money."

I finally realized that I couldn't talk to this person any longer. I managed to politely (just barely) thank him for calling and I hung up. It was clear that we weren't communicating, or if we were, he wasn't going to do anything anyhow. We were obviously coming from two different planets when it came to the issue at hand. When I hear people talk about "owning" a dog, I understand that they've missed the point entirely. You don't "own" a dog. The whole concept implies subservience and a "thing" mentality. You own inanimate objects, not living beings. And, to attach a monetary value on a dog because he or she is a "purebred" makes no sense to me at all. I'd blown it big time.

I didn't care about the illegal issue in terms of my taking him from the premises. Nothing would come of that. The people wouldn't dare pursue the point when they were so obviously negligent. I did care about the fact that Casper had trusted me to do the right thing for him, and I hadn't helped him at all. He was right back in that cold, wet cage. They'd obviously gone to get him when I was out running errands and because the pen was in the back of their house, I didn't know he was there.

Now what? What could I do? Could I sneak over in the middle of the night and steal him? What would that accomplish? I'd have the dog, but what would I do with him? I certainly couldn't (and wouldn't) bring him back to the shelter. Even though I knew that he was well cared for there, after talking with the animal control officer, I realized that the shelter's hands were tied up in legalities and they had no choice but to return him to the people who came to get him. Should I talk to the people again? Could I convince them to give him up? Not likely. If they viewed him as a pure-bred possession, they had probably paid quite a bit of money for him and wouldn't give him away. Maybe I could offer to buy him. Maybe money was the answer.

With that thought in mind, I marched across the street and knocked on the door. This time a woman answered. I introduced myself and told her that I understood Casper was back with them. Before she had a chance to respond, I told her that I'd like to buy him and would pay whatever price she named. She didn't invite me in, but instead closed the door so we were both standing outside. She apologized for having us stand outside in the cold, but she explained that she didn't want the kids to hear our conversation. She went on to say that she couldn't sell Casper to me because he "belonged" to the kids and they didn't want to give him up. She said they had insisted that he be brought home from the shelter and they were happy he was home.

"Where is he?"

"Who? Oh, you mean Casper? He's in his kennel."

Take a deep breath. Count to ten. "Do you have any idea how cold it is outside? How can you allow him to be out in this weather? If the kids are so happy he's home, why isn't he inside the house with them?"

"Oh, we don't allow him in the house. My husband built that nice kennel for him outside and he has his own dog house. The kids go out and visit him. And they take him for walks. He's perfectly happy there."

Yeah, right. "That's funny. You've lived here, what, two weeks now, and I've never seen the kids walking him. In fact, I didn't even know he was here. How often do they go out and visit him? Have you seen the inside of the pen?" I was losing my patience and politeness was about to be thrown out the window.

"Well, they take him his food in the morning. But, it's pretty cold for the kids to be outside and so they don't go out there much in this weather. They were supposed to clean his kennel and feed him before we left, but I guess they forgot. You know how kids are. But, he's fine. He has a nice large kennel."

I'd heard enough. It was time to be blunt. "Look, I know that I have no right to tell you what to do, but you're not taking care of Casper. And, you certainly haven't taught your kids anything about taking care of him. Telling me that you can't sell him to me because he belongs to the kids is a cop out. The pen is a pigsty, and it didn't get that way overnight. The blanket in the dog house is soaking wet and covered with maggots. His coat was matted and tangled. He's so thin he'll die if you leave him outside. He deserves to live with you as a member of your family. If you aren't willing to love him and keep him safe and warm, please, please, sell him to me. I'll find a home for him. There were several people who came to the shelter and wanted to adopt him. Please. Don't do this to him."

By this time I was in tears, but the woman was unmoved. "I think you'd better go now. Casper isn't for sale."

Once more, I turned away and went home. I wanted to go out and talk to Casper but I didn't know what I could say to him that would make any sense, and I couldn't tolerate seeing him back in that hole. There was nothing more I could do. I felt awful. I felt worse than awful. It was a long, long night.

The next day I saw the animal control truck across the street. It was there for maybe ten minutes. So much for education and the rights of a neglected animal. I was irate as I jumped in our car and followed the truck. I figured he was probably going to the shelter, so I would have a few minutes to get my anger under control. As the animal control officer was getting out of the truck at the shelter, I went over and introduced myself.

"I noticed that you did go to Casper's house, but you were there such a short time. Wasn't anyone home?"

"Oh, sure, they were home. We had a talk and everything's going to be fine now. Don't worry about it. The dog isn't your responsibility."

"How could you hope to educate them in ten minutes? Did you see the pen? What did you tell them?"

"Yes, I saw the kennel. I told them they needed to put straw on the floor and inside the dog house so it would be warmer for the dog. I told them they needed to make an appointment to have him neutered so he would gain some weight. The kennel was fine. There was no wet blanket. There wasn't any poop on the ground."

"Well, at least that's something. They knew you were coming and made some attempt to clean the place. But it won't last. You've condemned that dog to a life of hell. He's going to die out there in the cold. They don't care about him at all."

"Look, I've done what I could. He's their dog. They're providing what the law requires in terms of food, water and shelter. I'm working hard to change the county laws regarding animal welfare, but I can't do it alone. People need to get involved by writing letters and attending county commissioner meetings. There's nothing else I can do right now. I'd suggest that you back off. I'll be by to check on him periodically. Please understand that I feel as badly as you do about this. I wish your neighbors had surrendered him to the shelter so he could be adopted, but they didn't and so the shelter had no choice but to return him to them."

Once again, there was nothing else I could say. He went into the shelter and I got back in my car and returned home. It was over. The shelter had complied with county regulations by returning Casper to the people who had come to claim him, and the animal control officer had upheld a law that isn't strong enough to protect dogs like Casper.

Winter continued to work its cold magic on the island with more snow and freezing temperatures. There wasn't a day that I didn't think about Casper. I never saw anyone walking him. Often I'd spend hours in front of the window, sending him warmth through the power of my thoughts. I dreamed about him. They were nightmares. I tried to dream with him, but

I couldn't find him in my dreams. I felt him retreating farther and farther away.

One cold afternoon, many weeks after Casper had been returned to his pen, I was driving away from home when suddenly I started to shiver. I had warmed the car up before I left the garage and the heater was going full blast, but I felt so cold. Without warning, Casper's face appeared in front of me. He looked terrible and I could barely hear him. What I heard was just a whisper.

"Dale. Dale. Please come. Say goodbye."

I stopped the car and immediately turned around and drove into the driveway of Casper's house. Without giving a thought to consequences, I went directly behind the house to Casper's pen where I found him lying on the concrete. There was straw on the ground, but it was dirty and there was frozen poop everywhere. I quickly opened the gate, went inside, and gathered him up in my arms.

"Casper, please talk to me. I'm so sorry. Please forgive me. I'm going to take you out of here; I never should have let this happen. I've got to get you out of here right now. They'll never find you. Ever. Please hang on while I lift you up."

His voice was only a whisper. He was barely breathing. "Dale. Friend. It's okay."

"No, dear boy; it's not okay. Just hang on and I'll get you to the vet."

I took off my jacket and wrapped it around him as I picked him up and stumbled back to the car. I laid him in the back seat, jumped in and took off for the vet's office. As I drove, I kept talking to him, telling him to please stay with me. Needless to say, we made the five minute trip in about two minutes. I was in such a hurry that I would have welcomed a police escort.

After I squealed to a stop at the front door of the veterinary clinic, I raced around the car and lifted Casper out of the back seat. Ken must have heard my loud arrival because he had the door open for me before I even tried to open it myself, which would have been difficult at best under the circumstances.

Ken and I have known each other a long time and he knew that for me to arrive with an apparently unconscious animal in my arms meant serious business. He didn't waste time asking questions. He just said, "Tell me."

While we carried Casper to the surgery room, I gave him the short version. "He's almost frozen to death and he's hardly breathing. His gums are so white he must be in shock. I don't think we have much time."

"Okay. You get the large heating pad that's in the storage room. I'll start heating the fluid bag in the microwave."

I found the heating pad as well as a blanket that was on the shelf, and returned to the surgery room. Ken had put the bag of fluids in the microwave and while it was heating, he started the oxygen and placed a mask over Casper's nose. I plugged in the heating pad, set it to the highest temperature and we lifted Casper up so he could lie on the pad. I then covered him with the blanket and watched as Ken gave him an injection of a fast-acting steroid that would work with the fluids to open Casper's blood vessels. Ken was reaching for his stethoscope so he could listen to Casper's heart as the microwave beeped; I grabbed the bag of fluids, gave it to Ken and he started the I.V.

"How long has he been out in the cold?"

"It's a long story; I'll fill you in later. Let's help him if we can right now. I can't let him die. It's my fault he's in this horrible condition."

As I tucked the blanket closely around Casper, I begged him to stay with us. "Casper, I know you can hear me. Please hang on. You're going to be fine. I promise." After what I'd promised him weeks ago I don't know how I dared to promise him anything, but the words just spilled out of my mouth. Hopefully Ken would make it possible for me to keep my promise this time.

Ken looked at me and shook his head, but he kept working. He got the I.V. going and listened to Casper's heart while I held my breath, hoping I would hear Ken say that he still heard a heartbeat.

"His heart is still beating, but it's slow and weak. I don't know, Dale. He may not make it. We'll have to wait and see if he responds to the heat, fluids and steroids. He's pretty shocky."

Just for added measure, and because I needed to be as close as possible to Casper, I draped my body over him and hung on to him as tightly as I could without hurting him. While I stood there, I kept talking. But Casper didn't respond.

Finally, after what seemed like hours, but couldn't have been that long, I felt Casper stir beneath me. Not much movement, but enough to offer encouragement.

"Ken, he moved. Listen to his heart again. I think he's coming around."

Peeling away the blanket just enough to get his stethoscope in place, Ken listened. And, he smiled. "It's stronger. Not good yet, but better."

Yes!

For the next hour, I stayed with Casper while Ken attended to the clients who were stacked up by now in the waiting room. I could hear dogs and cats talking to each other, wondering when it would be their turn and wishing they could go home. Ken came in to check on Casper after he'd seen each patient, and each time he offered a bigger smile.

"Dale? Dale, is that you? Where … what's happening? Last thing … remember … calling you." Casper's voice was only a muffled whisper under the oxygen mask, but it was the most wonderful whisper I'd ever heard.

"Yeah, sweetheart. It's me. We're at the vet's office, and you're getting some oxygen, fluids and warmth to help you. Relax, you'll be fine. I'm right here."

"Okay. Feel better. Got cold and scared."

"I know, sweetie. I know. Just sleep if you can. You're a very brave boy."

Casper closed his eyes and slept while I found a chair and sat next to him. As I held his paw in my hand, I started to feel the anger I knew was lurking right below the surface of my consciousness, but I knew that I couldn't project that kind of energy right now so I stifled it and sent him loving and positive thoughts.

When Ken finally finished with his clients, he came in and checked Casper again. This time he removed the oxygen mask and pulled up another chair. "Okay, Dale. Want to tell me what's going on here?"

I told him the whole story from the time I'd first met Casper until our dramatic entrance into the clinic. He listened carefully, as he always does, and finally when my long saga- filled with much anger and regret- ended, he offered his thoughts.

"Well, it's obvious that his people haven't been taking care of him. He can't be outside in this weather. Do you want me to talk to them? They brought Casper in to be neutered awhile back, and I recognized him as Harold Winthrop's dog right away when you came into the clinic with him."

"Oh, I don't know, Ken. Will it do any good? It didn't make any difference when the animal control officer talked to them. I want him to be safe, warm and loved. I can't let him go back there again. I just can't."

"I know how you feel, Dale, but let me at least talk to Harold. This is obviously a case of severe neglect and I have to deal with it. I'll ask Harold to come in, and I'll also call animal control so Jeff Smithson can be here too for the meeting. Between the two of us maybe we can talk some sense into Harold. I'm going to make both calls right now because I want Harold to come in and see the dog right away. Now is a good time because I'm finished for the day. You can stay, but you have to promise to let me handle this. You're too angry to be helpful. Promise?"

I felt like picking up Casper and running, but I trust Ken and agreed to let him handle the situation. Once again I reminded myself that the objective was to help Casper, not to indulge myself in an angry rant.

Casper was stirring even more so I turned my attention back to him while Ken made the calls. "Hey, buddy. Are you feeling better?"

"Yeah. Home now?"

I almost couldn't believe what I was hearing, but I'd had enough experience with "battered child syndrome" to know that both children and animals are often intensely loyal to their people, no matter what kind of abuse they've suffered. "Do you really want to go back there? How could you, after they've neglected you so badly?"

"I guess. Maybe nice man and other guy can make it better. Maybe they don't mean it. Don't wanna be alone and cold."

I shook my head, marveling at the forgiving nature of this wonderful animal. "Okay, Casper, but I don't want to let you down again. I don't like this at all, but we'll see what your man has to say."

Ken came back in the room and said that he'd reached Animal Control Officer Smithson as well as Harold Winthrop. They would both be here in about fifteen minutes. I didn't ask what he'd said to them because the determined look on Ken's face told me all I needed to know.

More time passed as I sat with Casper and watched him sleep. Finally I heard the voices of the animal control officer and the man in Casper's house. They were out in the waiting room and I could hear Ken greeting them and asking both men to come into the surgery room.

When the three men came into the room I acknowledged both Mr. Winthrop and Officer Smithson with a nod, but I didn't say anything. I didn't move either. I wasn't about to leave Casper's side. At that moment, I was Mama Bear and Casper was my cub. Both men nodded back at me, and if they were surprised to see me there, they didn't reveal their feelings.

The meeting lasted for about half an hour and Ken was wonderful. He described the condition Casper had been in when we'd arrived, told them what he'd done to help him, and he was firm and forceful in his comments. Officer Smithson reminded Mr. Winthrop about the first time they'd met, and was aggressively direct as he expressed his disappointment that Casper hadn't received better care since then. He sounded as angry as I felt, but his anger carried more weight because he wore the badge. Casper watched and listened to the whole conversation, but his eyes mostly stayed on the man of the house. His man.

Finally, after much talk back and forth, it was agreed that Casper would return home with Mr. Winthrop and he would sleep in the house- at least for a couple of days until he was well- and then a place would be made for him in the garage. Mr. Winthrop even said that he would bring out a portable heater so the dog could stay warm. He also promised that he personally would take Casper for walks, see to it that he was well fed, and in general be responsible for improving his life.

None of this was good enough for me, but I kept my promise and didn't say anything. One of the options Ken had offered to Mr. Winthrop was for him to surrender Casper to the shelter and let them find a home for him, but the offer was refused. Mr. Winthrop was adamant about wanting another chance to make life more comfortable for Casper.

Casper left with Mr. Winthrop and went back home. I wasn't hopeful, but Casper seemed happy to be returning to his family; he smiled and gave me a weak "paws up" gesture as he was carried from the clinic by his man.

Harold Winthrop kept his promise. I didn't see Casper outside for several days, and when he did appear, he was on the end of a leash held by Harold. The next positive event I witnessed was a massive garage cleaning effort by the whole family. The garage was cleaned out, hosed down, and I saw a dog bed and blankets being brought out after the floor was dry. After a while, the weather turned warmer and Casper was back out in his pen, but when I walked by (I couldn't resist) the cage was clean, the water in his bowl was fresh, the dog house had dry blankets in it, and there wasn't any poop to be seen on the floor. There was also a tarp over the top of the cage to protect Casper from the rain.

Several months later the Winthrop family, including Casper, moved to a different town on the island and I never saw them again. Well, I never saw the people again, but I found out where they lived and I drove by often to check on Casper. He and I talked through the fence and he assured me that he was fine and that I wasn't to worry about him. He had gained weight, was clean, and even though he wasn't leading the kind of life I would have wished for him, he did seem safe and warm. Months later I found out that they had all moved to Palm Springs and their departure marked the end of my visits with Casper.

Palm Springs. Maybe Casper had a fenced yard with lush green grass and Palm trees to provide shade for him on warm days. I liked imagining him being so warm that he needed shade.

As I think about Casper and the lessons he's taught, I'm happy that he does have a more comfortable life, but he should never have had to suffer and almost die of neglect. The laws and county ordinances need to be changed. I also know that I will never again defer to the authorities if I see an animal in trouble. The animal's welfare must come first. Hopefully, some day soon, there will be enough support from a truly caring community to give voice to the needs and rights of animals. Support, followed by action, will then create a more humane society.

Show and Tell

"Show and Tell" was never this good when I was a kid.

The only time I remember anybody bringing an animal to school was the day that Jeff Vandenhoof brought his pet frog. He was allowed to have the frog as his "show and tell" if he promised not to let Hoppy out of his box. Unfortunately, Jeff didn't keep his promise, and Hoppy did his thing all around the classroom while most of the girls did what little girls do when they see a frog. The teacher, Jeff, and the rest of the boys chased Hoppy until they finally captured him and that was the end of anyone being able to bring animals to school.

The current thinking at the time was that animals didn't belong in a classroom. I've always liked seeing animals in classrooms, but then I like seeing animals everywhere. People who attend my college classes are encouraged to bring their dogs and often there are several canine companions in attendance. I don't think the dogs care much about learning psychology, and they often sleep during our discussions, which probably says something important about the validity of the subject matter, but I like having them there. They reinforce the 'oneness' of the experience.

I also like what I'm seeing in the fifth grade classroom I'm visiting today. I've been invited to sit in on the day's "show and tell" experience because my friend Barb is bringing her two animal friends as her granddaughter's contribution. I've stuffed myself into a desk at the back of the room that wasn't designed for adults and I'm watching the show. What a great show it is.

I came at the beginning of the class so I wouldn't interrupt anyone, and there were several presentations before the one I'd come to see. One girl brought her favorite stuffed animal, a dinosaur. She told the class all about her friend Dino and why he was so important to her. When she was ill last year, her parents had bought Dino for her as a comforting present and she said he was so soft and cuddly he made her feel better. Dino is pretty tattered and worn, but he's clearly a prized possession. Another student brought his favorite deck of cards with him and proceeded to dazzle the class (and me) with magic tricks. I'm still trying to figure out how he did most of them. Finally it was time for the dogs.

Barb waited outside the classroom until it was time for Tigger and Sam to make their entrance, and when it was her turn, Julie, Barb's granddaughter, went to the door and she and Barb brought the two dogs into the room. I was interested to see how the kids reacted when a large retired racing Greyhound and a Pointer entered the room. The teacher had told the kids to stay in their seats, but I could see that it was difficult for some of them to follow her instructions. They'd been told that they could pet the dogs later, but later wasn't soon enough. Later isn't ever soon enough for kids. They did comply though and kept their seats as Julie and Barb brought Tigger and Sam to the front of the room.

The kids probably would have been quiet and respectful for any guest speaker, but when the guests were dogs that they hadn't seen before, the students were delighted. Many of the students lived with dogs, a fact that had been established before the dogs were brought in, but all of them said that they'd never seen a Greyhound up close and none of them knew that there was a dog called a Pointer.

Tigger, always dignified and polite, quietly stood next to Barb, while Sam moved back and forth at the end of the leash Julie was holding, straining to get closer to the kids in the first row. Both dogs were used to being around kids, and they took this room full of twenty-five in stride as they waited for the introductions to begin. As I watched the kids, I noticed that every single one of them was smiling. They liked what they saw and connected immediately. I could tell that these were kids who were kind to animals. There's something about the way some kids and dogs respond to each other that's reassuring and comfortable.

The teacher asked Julie to introduce the dogs and tell the class about them, so she began with Sam. "Sam is my grandma's dog and he's almost three years old. He's called a Pointer because he's a hunting dog. He used to live in Alabama, but he ran away from his man because the man was mean to him and hit him. He even has scars on his head from where the man hit him. He got taken to a dog shelter and some people bailed him out and took him to Mississippi. The place he stayed in Mississippi couldn't keep him, so somebody brought him to Florida and that's where he was when my grandma saw his picture on the Internet. He flew in an airplane all the way from Florida to here and now he has a real home."

While Julie talked, Sam sat quietly and looked up at her with obvious approval. And when Julie told the class about his having a real home now, he went over to Barb and licked her hand.

"I never heard of a dog flying on an airplane. Sam, did you get to sit in a seat like everybody else?" This question came from a girl in the second row. Kids (and some adults) know that they can talk to dogs and so she understood that she could direct her question to him. "Weren't you scared? I flew in an airplane once and I was sorta scared."

Sam looked around and found the girl who'd asked the question and sat down to answer her. "Well, the plane ride wasn't so scary, but what happened before was really awful. When the humans brought me out to the airplane, they used a kind of fork lift thing and the guy who was operating it didn't do it right and I got dropped. When I fell, my crate broke open and I was so scared I just ran. I didn't know where I was and it was so noisy with the planes and all that I panicked. All I could do was run and nobody could catch me."

I'd heard this story before, but as I watched the kids I could see that they were horrified. Some of them fired questions before they remembered to raise their hands. "Oh, Sam." "That's awful." "What did you do?" "Where did you go?" "How did they finally get you?" "Didn't you get hurt running around there?"

"I was on the run for two days before the police found me. I even had to cross six lanes of traffic on the Miami Freeway to get to the other side. It was so hot my paw pads had blisters by the time I got found. When the police finally caught me they had to surround me. I felt kinda like a criminal, but way down deep I was sure glad to stop running. I didn't know where they were gonna take me, but I figured anything had to be better than running and hiding. Somebody got a hold of the lady who'd brought me to the airport, and so she came to get me and kept me at her house before I flew away for real."

"This time she made sure I got on the plane okay, and there was somebody waiting at the other end who took me off the plane and brought me to Barb and Ron. I'm okay now, but I still have nightmares sometimes. When I first came I was scared when the planes would fly over our house, but now I run around in the yard and bark at them."

Very much aware that Sam was her "show and tell," Julie wanted to say more about Sam. Maybe she figured that she was the one getting the grade and so she should do most of the talking. "Sam's a great dog. He's really friendly, and he thinks that it's his job to keep my grandma and grandpa's yard safe from squirrels and deer. He likes to run too; they take him a couple of times a week to that fenced dog park where dogs can run free. Boy, is he fast! I think that guy who was mean to him must have hit him with a stick or something because when anybody comes near him with a broom or a mop, he shakes all over and tries to hide. Poor guy has had a hard time, but he's okay now."

The teacher, wanting to keep things moving, then suggested to Julie that she let her grandma hold Sam while she told the class about Tigger. Only too happy to oblige, Julie gave

Sam's leash to Barb, took Tigger from her and walked over to the center of the room. Tigger is such a large Greyhound that he stood taller than Julie. His beautiful brindle coat is shiny and even though he seems thin, I knew that he'd gone from a racing weight of seventy-one pounds to a healthy eighty-six pounds since he'd come to live with Barb and her husband. Now he has muscles instead of ribs sticking out.

Julie was ready to talk about Tigger. "Tigger is a Greyhound that used to race on a track. His racing name was Peacock Rain, but I like Tigger much better. I used to think it was neat that he was a racing dog, but my grandma told me that it's an awful life for a dog, and it's good that he doesn't have to do that anymore. She said that if the dogs don't win enough they're retired and if they don't get adopted they get killed. No matter how old they are. Tigger is two and he would've been killed if he hadn't been rescued."

I know that Greyhound rescue groups all over the country try to rescue as many dogs as they can. Often, if dogs race at what they call a Class D racetrack, they're in real danger. When they don't win enough, they're electrocuted and their bodies are thrown away at a local dump site. To say that racing Greyhounds are used, exploited and then thrown away if they aren't rescued is an understatement. Tigger was one of the fortunate ones that'd been rescued and then adopted by Barb and Ron.

Telling her classmates that dogs that don't perform get killed was a significant statement for Julie to make to the class. Some might think that kids don't need to hear unsettling information like this, but I think it's important for them to hear the truth. They need to know that humans take advantage of animals in order to make money. I made a mental note to ask the teacher after class if her students could talk with someone who would tell them about the abuses involved in using animals for the circus too. My thoughts were interrupted by Tigger who wanted to speak for himself.

"I sure am glad to be here and to have such a great home. Where I live there are lots of soft cushions all around the house, which is great because I don't have much skin on my joints. Having a soft bed is important to me.

I guess you could say that I'm kind of a couch potato. It's a big change from being in a cage all the time. I get to really stretch out."

A boy sitting in front of me raised his hand. "Hey, Tigger, do they call you that 'cuz you jump up a lot?"

Tigger smiled and responded. "Well, I guess, and because I have stripes. I'm not huggy like Sam here, and so when my people come home after they've been gone awhile, I jump straight up in the air. It's my way of showing them that I love them and am happy to see them. Barb and Ron say that I'm shy and sensitive. But, I have a great smile. See?"

When Tigger smiled for the class, everyone applauded and gave him their biggest smiles in return.

"Do you guys wanna hear about how my grandma and grandpa found Tigger?" Julie wanted the floor back. Her question was met with a chorus of eager voices.

"Yeah, tell us." "How'd they get him?"

"Well, they knew they wanted to adopt a Greyhound so they read lots of books and talked to some people in town who rescue them. The people came out to their house to make sure they had a safe place for a dog, and then they called later and told them some new dogs were coming in and they should come and see. When they went to this place, there were lots of Greyhounds there in a big pen. When they walked into the pen, this one big dog came right over and glued himself to my grandpa's leg. That was Tigger. He knew that they were his people. He's shy too, and you can't talk loud around him or he'll go away. I think he was yelled at a lot when he was racing and he can't stand loud noises. He likes to lie around the house. He's really a neat dog."

I saw the teacher looking at her watch and I knew that class would be over soon. The kids knew it too, and a girl in the front row asked if it was time for them to be able to pet the dogs. Rather than having them all crowd around the dogs in the front of the room, the teacher suggested that Barb and Julie walk the dogs up and down each row so everyone would get a chance to touch them.

It was a wonderful sight to see these two dogs that'd had such terrible beginnings to their lives be so well adjusted and secure that they could receive the kindness and respect of young strangers. Tigger was reserved as he walked, and the kids sensed his shyness. They touched him gently and with respect. Sam, on the other hand, didn't have any strangers in his life, and he greeted everyone with enthusiasm as they patted him and hugged him.

The petting parade finished as the bell rang. After the teacher thanked everyone for their presentations, she dismissed the class and they all went roaring off for their lunch break. Julie left with the other students after she gave Tigger and Sam hugs and thanked them for being her "Show and Tell." As she raced out the door she told her grandma that she'd see her on Sunday for dinner.

The teacher needed her lunch too, but I took a moment to ask her if she'd be willing to have someone come in and talk to the class about how circus animals are treated. She said she knew just the person to call and agreed to set something up. She then thanked Barb for bringing the dogs and left to get her lunch.

As Barb and I walked to her car with Sam and Tigger, I suggested that the boys might like a little run after their teaching session and we agreed to meet at the closest off-leash park. I followed in my own car and met them at the nearby park.

Once off leash and safe in the enclosed area created to let dogs run free, Sam and Tigger raced away at top speed. Tigger easily passed Sam as we watched and Barb explained that when Tigger first came to them, he always ran in a circle as if he were running on a track. She added that he's learned from Sam that he isn't on a track any longer so when Sam gets close to him, he turns and gallops away in the other direction. He was doing that very thing as we stood there. Tigger's agility and grace of movement was amazing.

Barb shook her head as she watched them. "It's such a shame what society has done in terms of breeding, isn't it? Take Sam, for example. He's been bred to react in a certain, circumscribed manner in order to fulfill his role in humans' grand design. He's been bred to run, and ideally he's best suited to hunting with a rider on horseback. Fortunately, we can give him plenty of exercise, both here and in the yard at home, but what happens to the other dogs of his breed when they end up in circumstances that don't match their needs? Never mind, I know the answer. Tigger was bred to race and thrown away when he wasn't useful any more. Pretty sad commentary on expendable animals isn't it?"

"True, but fortunately there are people like you and Ron who are willing to adopt rescued animals. Hopefully Greyhound racing will eventually be banned, and perhaps without so much emphasis on breeding, and more emphasis on spaying and neutering, some kind of balance can be achieved."

Tigger and Sam screeched to a stop in front of us. They'd been running non- stop since we arrived and they weren't even out of breath. Sam came over for a hug. "Hey, what're you guys talking about? You look so serious. We're here to have some fun. Be in the moment, ladies. Be in the moment." And with that bit of wisdom, he raced off.

Tigger started to go after him, but came back to Barb and gave her an awesome smile. "He's right, you know. We did some good teaching today. Those kids heard what we had to say and they'll tell their parents about the class, and maybe the parents will tell their friends, and then their friends will tell other people, and before you know it, change happens. For now, lighten up, ladies. Catch us if you can."

Catch them? Yeah, right. That'd be the day. The two of us running after dogs that were in better shape than we'd be in six lifetimes would be enough of an event to warrant calling the paramedics. Besides, watching these two beautiful animals was much more fun than running any day. Watching them allowed us to appreciate their grace, exuberance and sense of freedom. Knowing that Tigger wasn't being forced to race any more gave us the pleasure of watching him run for the sheer joy of the experience. And, knowing that Sam didn't have to run away from abuse and danger any more gave us the pleasure of watching him run just for fun.

As it should be.

An Elephant Named Sonny

"Hey, guys, remember Sonny the elephant?"

Pip, Fitz, and Joey were doing their Schnauzer lounge on the deck when I joined them, carrying a letter that had just come in the mail.

"He was huge! Biggest animal I ever saw." "Even though we only saw him from the motor home window, I couldn't believe how big he was." "Wow! Sure, we remember him. What about him?"

"Well, this letter tells us that he died. All of his friends at Popcorn Park are having a memorial service for him next week. I'm so glad we got to see him when we did, but I wish we could go to the service."

Pip looked at me like I'd lost my mind. "Why? Why do we need to go somewhere else to remember him? We can remember him right here. He'll hear us. You know that, Dale."

"I know. You're right, Pip, but it seems like we should be there with everyone else who loved him. You know, to pay our respects."

"But, Dale, didn't we pay our respects to him when we met him last October? Seems like you said that's why we were there. We drove almost 4,000 miles to see him. That seems pretty respectful to me."

Joey, ever the curious one, had a question. "So, how come he was in that place? You never told us that. Why wasn't he with his family?"

I knew that being without his family was incomprehensible to Joey, so I pulled him closer and answered his question. "I know, Joey. It was hard to see him without his herd, but let me tell you how he got there. Remember how you felt when you were separated from your family and ended up at the shelter?"

"Yeah, I felt sad and scared. One day I had a family and then before I knew what was going on, they didn't want me any more. I never got what happened, but you took me out of that place and now everything is okay again. Is that what happened to Sonny?"

"No, sweetie. What happened to Sonny is even more horrible than what happened to you. When he was about two years old, Sonny, along with lots of other young elephants, was forcibly taken from his home in a place called Zimbabwe. One day while he was playing near a river with his herd, humans came after him. He had to watch as his whole family was destroyed. After the humans killed his family, they captured him"

"But, why?" Fitz was incredulous. "Why would humans do such an awful thing?"

"They wanted to use and exploit him. Humans use elephants in circuses. They keep them in zoos. They march them in parades. They use them in movies. They kill them and use their tusk ivory for jewelry. I even saw an elephant foot once that was used as the base of a table. Unfortunately, humans do terrible things to elephants … and to other animals too. Right, Pip?

Pip, whose spine was cracked when she first came to us because she'd been beaten so badly, nodded her head. "Yes, Dale. But, I try not to think of that time anymore. Did Sonny get hurt too? I mean physically?"

"Yes, Pip. When the humans captured him they treated him roughly and his trunk was badly torn. He was beside himself with grief and the humans had a hard time controlling him."

"I know the feeling." Pip was remembering that she herself was a frightened wild thing when we rescued her. "But, how did Sonny get from where he was captured to that place in New Jersey where we saw him, Dale?"

"Well, he was moved from one zoo to another, but he was a rogue elephant that couldn't fit in anywhere. He eventually went to a small zoo in New Mexico, but he kept escaping. They couldn't care for him and so they decided to kill him to put him out of his misery."

Joey was disgusted. "Let me see if I've got this straight. Humans made him miserable and lonely to begin with by killing his family and capturing him, and then they were gonna put him out of the misery that they created for him by killing him? Is that stupid or what?"

"Well, I think I'd use a stronger word than 'stupid,' but fortunately, this place in New Jersey, called Popcorn Park, operated by The Associated Humane Societies, heard about Sonny and opened their gates to him. That's where we saw him. It's a shelter, but they take in big animals too."

"I hate shelters." Joey was adamant on the subject. "They're scary places. Wasn't he scared there?"

"Yeah, at first he was. But John, the zoo director, took care of him and became his friend. He helped Sonny learn to trust humans. John would stay up late with Sonny if he didn't feel well. He even brought his sleeping bag into Sonny's compound and slept near him. Because Sonny knew that John loved him, he gradually accepted the love and respect that everyone at Popcorn Park gave him. And he was given the best possible care. Volunteers built a huge compound for him; he had lots of fruits and vegetables to eat, and he eventually learned to trust people because he understood that everyone there was totally devoted to his well-being. They couldn't give him his freedom, but they could, and did, give him love and respect."

"I guess he didn't die without being loved by people, did he? It would've been sad if he'd never felt what it was like to have a human love him. We know how important being loved is, don't we guys?" Fitz moved over closer to Joey and Pip as he asked his question.

All three snuggled closer to me in answer to Fitz's question. No response necessary.

Later that night I thought about our meeting with Sonny. Even though Ellaine and I had been sponsoring him ever since he came to Popcorn Park twelve years ago, we'd never actually met him until we made the cross-country trip in October. When we arrived at Popcorn Park, we went into the office and told them who we were and why we were there. The women in the office were happy to meet us and directed us to Sonny's compound.

When we approached the large area that had been built for Sonny, we could see him way in the back, eating some vegetables. There was a fence bordering the compound so we couldn't get inside, but we called to him and asked him to come over and meet us. He looked up and slowly made his way over to the fence. There was a dry moat between the fence and where he stood, but he got as close as he could so we could talk.

"Hi handsome, it's so good to finally see you. We think about you all the time. I'm Dale, and this is my partner, Ellaine. We adopted you twelve years ago when you came here, and we're very proud that you're our boy. We love you."

Sonny lifted his trunk and wiggled those magnificent ears at us. "Hi Dale and Ellaine; I know who you are. You're the ones who dream with me. I recognize you from my dreams. It's nice to see you."

"It's wonderful to see you too. How're you doing? I know it must be hard for you not to be free and with your herd. I'm so sorry about what happened to you. Sometimes I feel ashamed to be human."

"I'm fine, Dale. My friend John has helped me. And everyone here is so good to me. They treat me with respect. I'm used to being confined, and I'm not always sad anymore. I've learned that all humans aren't bad. That's a good thing to learn. And, I'm teaching people too by being here. The words written on the fence tell everyone who comes here what happened to me and why I'm here."

We'd noticed the sign on Sonny's fence, and it was true that his story was told in detail so that people would know about the horrors and in-dignities that he'd suffered before he came to Popcorn Park. How sad that some lessons are taught at the expense of freedom and dignity. When will we ever learn?

"Kind ladies, what do you think of this place?"

"Well, Sonny, we have mixed feelings. We hate seeing all of the animals in captivity. Especially you. But, we're glad that you're all safe and pro-tected. And, I notice that there are signs everywhere telling people about all of the animals and how they came to be here. I guess the price of your freedom is that you get to teach people. I understand that."

"Yes, it's a big price to pay. I think people need to actually see us to understand. More people should come here. I'm glad you came to see me. I enjoy our dreams."

"Me too, my friend. Me too. You're so handsome, you know? I've never seen an elephant up close before because we won't go to zoos. I wish we could touch you. You're so beautiful."

"Thanks. Most people don't tell me I'm handsome or beautiful. I don't always feel that way, but when John and the others who work here look at me, like you're looking at me now, I can see how they feel and then I feel good too. I can tell that you see who I really am and I appreciate that. Lots of people come here and stare, without talking to me or looking at me. I know that they don't always know what to say, and sometimes I feel their sadness for me, but I like feeling respected too. I like feeling that I make a difference in people's lives. Don't worry about not being able to touch me. We're touching right now in the most important way. You know what I mean."

I did know what he meant. We were separated by physical distance, but we were close in spirit and in love.

I asked him if he'd mind if we took some photographs of him and when he said he didn't mind at all, we spent quite awhile talking with him and taking pictures of that magnificent displaced pachyderm. He even posed for us and I saw a hint of a smile now and then as he waved his trunk and wiggled his ears.

As I remembered our meeting, again I had mixed feelings. On the one hand I was happy for Sonny that he was finally free and at peace. I also felt such anger at the humans who had killed his family and made him suffer the indignities that had changed and shortened his life. (He was only twenty-one years old when he died; African elephants generally live fifty or sixty years.) But, I also felt gratitude for those at Popcorn Park, especially John, who had loved him and had treated him with compassion and respect.

For several days after Sonny's death, I wasn't able to dream with him. I kept looking for him, but I couldn't find him. I also wondered why I hadn't felt his death, or why I hadn't been able to dream with him after he died.

Finally, last night I dreamed with Sonny and understood. When he was at Popcorn Park, I dreamed with him to help him cope with his confinement and as a way for me to feel close to him. We had wonderful times together in those dreams, but other elephants were never a part of them.

In last night's dream, I found myself at the edge of a river. I saw Sonny move in a kind of graceful ballet with his mother and his herd. They danced together and the sense of freedom that surrounded them was palpable. He was healthy, happy, and his trunk wasn't torn. As I watched them move together, I felt the joy of freedom that he was finally able to experience. When he saw me, Sonny lifted his head and his trunk to the sky and I knew he was Home.

We didn't go to the memorial service, but we were told that more than 150 people attended to say their farewells to Sonny. People talked about him at the service and then afterward everyone went back to Popcorn Park to gather at Sonny's compound as bagpipes were played in his honor.

Trying to find a way to deal with their grief, humane society staff contacted Colleen Nicholson, an animal wellness consultant who communicates with animals after they've gone Home. Colleen heard Sonny and was able to pass his message on to John and everyone who loved him. Sonny's message is clear, and this story ends with his words.

Thank you, Sonny.

"The work we have done can be a model to your world. Chronicled and recorded, it can show that the life of an elephant is a great tribulation for Earth. From the largest being to the smallest, there is a purpose and a meaning for each. From the smallest to the largest, there is a right for each to exist. Each being comes to Earth with a purpose before him. Each being is a reflection of a greater truth. Sadly, many humans must have forgotten."

"The greatest memorial to me that you can give is that of my story to the world. Help others learn that we are all connected in life. And the tears you shed as you speak will not fall hard upon your face because I will be by your side, lifting my trunk to wipe your horrors away as you once did mine. And hear my trumpeting in the wind for this is where I now reside."

160

Here's Lookin' At You, Kid!

Pathetic. That's the first word that came to mind when I saw his photograph on the shelter website. His scrawny black body was draped over the arms of a shelter volunteer and his pale blue cataract eyes glowed like iridescent contact lenses. Big Yoda ears stuck out in two different directions and he wasn't smiling at all. Not even a little bit. This little guy was clearly sad, lonely and lethargic. He didn't look like he had the energy to do much of anything except hope, and maybe not even much of that.

We knew that our Jenny would send someone to us after she went Home, and so looking at various shelter websites had become a common practice as we waited for our new friend to become known to us. On this particular day, the photograph of Angus appeared on the site of the Happy Hills Animal Foundation in North Carolina.

North Carolina? My heart sank as I read the location. No way. I'd heard all of the horror stories about what happened to dogs when they were shipped in planes, and I couldn't even imagine subjecting a blind caged animal to a plane flight. This couldn't be the one. Move on.

Over the next few weeks, more websites were checked, but we kept thinking about Angus. Blind, lonely, sitting in a cage waiting and hoping someone would choose him, even though he was described as being seven or eight years old. (Unfortunately, many people don't want to adopt an older dog. Their loss.) Maybe someone local would see beyond his disability and adopt him. Maybe someone wouldn't mind that he was older. Maybe someone would love him. Maybe …

One night in March before I fell asleep, I asked Jenny to dream with me and tell me who needed to come and live with us. That night I dreamed about Angus. I saw him here. I saw him smiling and I realized with absolute clarity that the someone Angus was waiting for was us. When I woke in the morning, I talked with Ellaine about my dream; we put aside our fears about plane travel for dogs and called Happy Hills.

I spoke to Becky who assured me that Angus was still there and didn't have anyone interested in him. She said that someone had adopted him, briefly, but had returned him because there was another older dog in the house that was so upset by Angus's presence that he'd stopped eating. Even though he thought Angus was a terrific dog, his adopter didn't feel he could jeopardize the health of his older dog for Angus. She also said that Angus had been found wandering the streets in early January and had been taken to the local pound where he was scheduled to be killed in seventy-two hours because he had no identification, no rabies tag, and no one had come to claim him. Happy Hills rescued him, had him neutered, gave him his shots and made him available for adoption. Becky added that they all thought Angus was a wonderful dog and he'd charmed his way into their hearts.

I expressed my concerns about shipping, and when I explained that we were in Washington state, Becky understood my hesitation and admitted that she had reservations too because they'd never shipped a dog so far away before.

"Okay, Becky, let me do some research, and if I can find a direct flight from somewhere in North Carolina to Seattle, can you get him to the airport?"

"You bet. We'll get him there. The closest airport to us is Raleigh, but I don't think they fly directly to Seattle, so you might have to see about Charlotte."

I told her I'd start checking and get back to her later in the day. After I hung up I called our local travel agent, and he said that he thought U.S. Airways flew directly from Charlotte to Seattle. While I waited, he checked and found that they did have a direct flight. I called the airlines and talked with someone who gave me information about what needed to happen in order for Angus to fly home to us. I didn't like the idea of putting a blind dog in a cage in the cargo hold of an airplane for five or six hours, but I kept my anxiety level down while getting more information. I even asked if Angus could travel in the passenger area with me. I was willing to fly to Charlotte and bring him back with me on a return flight, but I was told that if his crate wouldn't fit under the seat he had to fly in the temperature controlled cargo compartment. Only small dogs that fit in small crates could be in the passenger seating area. I had to have faith that he would be fine. If this was meant to be, we had to make it happen.

Many phone calls later, having been reassured by everyone with whom I spoke at the airlines that Angus would be well cared for, I called Happy Hills and told them what I'd learned. Becky said they'd send an adoption contract right out to us so we could formalize the process. I also asked Becky to please go out to Angus and tell him that we loved him already and that he'd be with us soon. She said she'd do that and before I hung up I added that I'd send a sign I wanted them to tape on his crate telling the airline attendants that he was precious cargo and to take very good care of him.

On March 22 Angus arrived in Seattle. We were at the airport early, pacing while we waited for his flight to land and for him to be delivered to us. We were so anxious to get him out of his crate, I practically ripped the crate containing our boy from the arms of the attendant who brought him through the double doors in the baggage claim area. We immediately opened the crate door and scooped him up.

"Hi Angus, welcome home, sweetheart."

Big smile, wet kisses and lots of tail wagging. "Hi y'all. It's okay. Ah'm fine. Boy, do ah have to pee. Kin we go outside?"

Southern accent? Of course. I'd forgotten that when I spoke with the ladies at Happy Hills they'd all talked with a soft southern drawl. No reason why dog-talk should be any different.

While Ellaine took Angus outside to relieve his bladder, I found the nearest phone and called Happy Hills to let them know that he'd arrived safely. Cheryl, the owner, had personally driven him all the way to Charlotte early in the morning, and I knew she and her staff were anxious to hear that he'd arrived safely. The phone only rang once; I knew they were watching the clock and waiting by the telephone. Any dog fortunate enough to end up at Happy Hills while waiting for a permanent home couldn't ask for more caring people. Once the message had been delivered, I joined Angus and Ellaine outside so I could get a closer look at our new friend.

He was so skinny his ribs showed and his backbone stuck out. I knew that Happy Hills had taken good care of him, but without a real home and a family of his own, Angus hadn't thrived. No more so than any of the dogs I've met at our local shelter. Now that he was here, he'd gain weight and be fine. Cheryl and her staff had kept him sane and that was enough for him during that time of his life.

The airport was noisy and unfamiliar to Angus and it was time to get home. I picked Angus up and carried him back to the truck to meet his Schnauzer brothers and sister. Joey and Fitz greeted their new brother enthusiastically and Pip, our matriarchal curmudgeon, looked at him and rolled her eyes.

"Is he gonna live with us?"

"Yes, Pip. I told you that on the way to the airport. His name is Angus. He's come all the way from North Carolina to be here. Please be nice."

"Hey, he can't see and he talks funny."

"Yeah, Joey. He has kind of a southern accent right now. That won't last long once he starts listening to you guys. Because he's blind, you're going to have to help him out until he settles in, okay?"

"That's fine. We'll take care of him." Fitz, ever the gentleman, was our resident caregiver.

"Okay guys, let's hit the road and get home before we get caught in traffic."

Once we were in the truck, the dogs sorted themselves out and Angus curled up on Ellaine's lap and went to sleep. Three hours later, after a long drive and a ferry ride, we were finally almost home. Angus had been in some kind of moving vehicle for about ten hours, considering his long drive to the airport in North Carolina, the plane flight, and now the drive home, but he wasn't bothered at all. The resiliency of shelter dogs never ceases to amaze me. They're so flexible and can adjust to almost any situation.

When we arrived home, I lifted Angus out of the truck and put him in the yard with the rest of the guys. Because he couldn't see, he bumped into everything, but we let him find his way, knowing that it wouldn't take long for him to become acclimated to his new surroundings. Fitz stayed close to Angus, acting as his own personal herder. After Angus explored the yard, we invited him into the house and let him wander around, sniffing and listening to his new home. We served him some dinner, which he ate in about three seconds flat, and then went about our business, talking to him the whole time so he knew where we were.

It took about two days for Angus to be able to go in and out of the house by himself and to be able to run around in the garden without bumping into anything that would hurt him. It was obvious that he was completely blind, but that didn't stop him from exploring. He told us that he'd been blind since he'd been born; that made sense because his ability to cope was off the scale. The more secure he felt, the more his internal radar clicked in and he began to sense how close he was to something before he bumped into it.

The people at Happy Hills had said that he loved to play in the water with the hose, so when we took him for his first walk on the beach, we were eager to see what he thought about the big waters of Puget Sound. I'd purchased a long flexi leash so he could run and play but still be safe with me on the other end. When I led him down to the water's edge, he went nuts.

"Wow! Holy Cow! What's this? Where's the hose that goes with this water? I wanna get wet. Let's go in the water. C'mon, Dale. Let's go!"

Angus barked at the waves and ran up and down the beach, all four feet in the water and the rest of him soaking wet (me too) as he experienced his new playground. Joey raced along beside him, but Joey doesn't do water so he barely got wet while he cheered Angus on. Pip and Fitz watched from a distance, Pip muttering all the time about crazy dogs that like the water.

Our life with Angus took on a routine that was comfortable for him and for us. He was a joy to watch because he was so happy. He didn't care that he couldn't see. His southern accent disappeared within a few days. Quite adaptable, our new boy. When we talked, he assured me that he was fine now that he had a family.

"Trust me, Dale. I haven't ever been able to see with my eyes. I just hear and smell and I know about stuff. Works for me. Now it's good because I know where I live and you guys are my seeing-eye people. I know you won't let anything happen to me. It's perfect."

We thought life with Angus was perfect too until I took Angus in to meet our local vet. Ken said that he was in good health and probably was more like three years old than seven or eight, and when he examined his eyes he presented a new and awesome possibility. A possibility that might make perfect even more perfect.

"You know, Dale, I think those cataracts could be removed. I know of an ophthalmologist in Seattle who could do the job. Do you want a referral?"

"Absolutely. I know he's fine now, but if there's a chance that he might be able to see without any risk to him, then I think we need to offer him that opportunity. Angus, what do you think?"

"Well, gee, Dale, I don't know what to say. I don't know what it means to be able to see so I can't tell you what I think. If you want me to have the surgery, and you think it's a good idea, let's do it. Can't hurt anything. If it doesn't work, then I'm as good as I am now, which is pretty okay with me."

So, I called for an appointment, and all of us made the trip into Seattle to meet Dr. Tom Sullivan. Wonderful guy. He and his staff greeted Angus enthusiastically as Angus charmed everyone in the clinic. Tom examined Angus's eyes carefully before he gave his opinion. After the examination, he said that he wanted to run an ultrasound and an ERG to be sure that there wasn't any glaucoma or retinal damage, which would prevent the surgery from being successful. He also said that if test results were good, there was an eighty percent chance that Angus would be able to see after the cataracts were removed and new lenses were inserted.

When we returned home from our initial appointment, we had a family meeting to discuss the pros and cons of the surgery. When all was said and done, Angus decided (with Joey, Pip and Fitz supporting his decision) that we should give it a try, so I set up a time for him to have the necessary tests to be sure the surgery was possible.

The tests were run the next week and the prognosis was good. No glaucoma or retinal damage. Angus, blind from birth, would be able to see!

"Okay, buddy. Are you still up for this? You'll need to wear one of those Elizabethan collars for two weeks after the surgery to protect your eyes because you don't want to scratch those new lenses with your paws. I'm also going to have to put three different kinds of drops in your eyes three times a day for a while. Can you handle all of that?"

"Dale, believe me, I can handle anything. As long as I have a family who loves me, I'll be fine. Will we still get to go to the beach?"

"Well, you can't be near the water right away, but we'll still go for our walk every day. We'll walk on the inside path; that way you won't get sand or water in your eyes."

"Okay, then, let's go for it. Oh, I won't miss any meals will I?"

"No, funny boy. Business as usual. You'll just have to deal with the collar."

It was decided. The appointment was made, and we all settled down in a wonderful kind of anticipatory waiting mode until the surgery day. Speculating about what it would be like for a blind dog to suddenly be able to see was almost impossible for us. And, since the optic nerves hadn't ever been exercised, the messages sent to his brain might be a little confusing at first. We wondered what it would be like for him. He wondered too, but he took the whole prospect in stride, as he did everything else.

"Aren't you a little apprehensive, Angus? After all, you'll be dealing with a whole new world. Doesn't that scare you at all?"

"Scare me? Why would it scare me, Dale? I'll still be able to hear and smell. I've got those senses pretty well wired after all this time. And from what you say, it'll be like adding another sense. Nothing's lost. So what if I'm confused for a while. I spent a lot of time being confused before I came to live with you and I managed. Besides, you guys will help me. I know you will. Don't worry."

Once again I was reassured by the calm acceptance of an animal. They always get it. They're so clear about everything while we humans muddle around in a maze of uncertainty. They know that we're all one. No one does anything alone. Chalk up another *first light* experience.

Surgery day finally arrived. Angus and I left for Seattle early in the morning while Ellaine stayed home with the other guys. Angus was a little cranky because there'd been no morning treats, but I reassured him that he'd have something special when we got home. I explained about the anesthetic as well as other details and told him that he'd be staying with me right up until surgery. I reassured him that when he woke up, he'd be in my arms and the first face he saw would be mine. We laughed about the fact that I'd look fuzzy to him, but he said that since he hadn't ever seen me with his eyes it didn't matter if I looked fuzzy. He also said, bless his diplomatic heart, that my appearance didn't matter.

After we arrived at Dr. Sullivan's office, there was a long waiting period during which time I put drops in Angus's eyes every thirty minutes until they were ready for surgery. Finally it was time and I reluctantly handed Angus over to Nancy, who would be assisting with the surgery. I'd asked if I could be present during surgery, but that request wasn't honored because it was felt that my presence would make people nervous. I didn't debate the point since I wanted everyone to be focused on Angus, and if they didn't feel comfortable having me there, that was fine. I'd still be with Angus in my own way.

For the next hour I walked in the neighborhood. I'd brought a book to read, but I kept reading the same paragraph over and over. There's always a danger with anesthetic and even though my heart knew that everything would be fine, I felt like I needed to be with him in spirit as best I could.

So I walked and felt his presence with me as he slept and was given the gift of sight. The clinic was located in the University district of Seattle and as I walked I looked at houses and made up stories about the people who lived there. Too crowded for my tastes, but it was an interesting walk and it gave me an opportunity to be with Angus without any significant distractions.

I'd been told that the surgery would take about an hour and a half so I made my way back to the clinic and went inside to wait. Leah, the office manager, said she'd bring Angus out to me as soon as he was ready. For another fifteen minutes I thumbed through magazines and made friends with two cute Miniature Australian Shepherds named Kiwi and Frankie. They were there with their lady because Kiwi had an eye infection. Frankie told me that he didn't want to wait in the car because he needed to provide moral support for his sister. I kept looking at the clock and I knew I was driving Leah crazy, but eventually she went in the back and brought Angus out to me.

He was still sleeping, wrapped in a towel so he wouldn't get chills as the anesthetic wore off. I took our precious bundle from Leah and held him until he began to stir. The Elizabethan collar made it awkward to get close to his face, but I hugged him and held him in my arms while I laid my head on his back.

"Hey, little buddy. You awake? Let's see you."

He stirred and turned his body to face me. They'd had to shave off his bushy eyebrows to keep the surgery area sterile, and so he had a kind of surprised look on his face, but he was fine. "Hi Dale. S'you. Sleepy. Nice face. Kinda fuzzy. Let's go home. I'm hungry."

"Hi sweetie; yeah, it's me. I know I'm fuzzy, but your vision will clear after a while. We can't leave yet because Tom has to check your eyes a couple of times for the next two hours to be sure everything's okay. You just relax and wake up."

For the next two hours we sat in the waiting room while Angus woke up. Tom came out and checked his eyes several times and said everything looked good. Finally he said we could leave but we'd have to come back in the morning for a post-op visit. By this time Angus was fully awake and raring to go. I took him outside to pee and that was an awkward trip because he hadn't gotten the hang of how to move with the collar on yet, but he stumbled around and did his thing. I knew he could see because he didn't bump into the tree that was outside, but he was still wobbly and I was anxious to get him home.

The trip home was uneventful and long. We got caught in commuter traffic and it took forever, but finally we were on the ferry and soon we were home. Angus slept the whole time while I drove and talked to him. I kept my right arm on his body so he knew I was there.

When we arrived home Ellaine and the gang were waiting for us and everyone milled around Angus while he wandered in the yard and tried to figure out how to get up the stairs with that big collar around his head. How frustrating. He could see, but the collar impaired his peripheral vision to such an extent that he had kind of a tunnel view of things. Once again, he managed, and it didn't take long before he was moving around without knocking the collar into whatever was in his way.

We wanted to talk to him about what it was like to see, but in true Angus style, what he wanted to do was eat. I used a smaller dish than his regular one and elevated it on a book to make it easy for him to reach his food. Although the collar extended beyond the length of his face, he could get to the dish because it fit inside the cone. No problem. He dived right in as usual.

After we were all settled on the bed, he looked around and started to fill us in on what was up with his new world. "Well, it's weird. I mean, I don't exactly know how to explain it. I can see all of you, and I know it's you because you smell like you and I hear your voices and your barks, but I don't know what any of it means. I'll get the hang of it, but my eyes kinda itch and I'm sleepy again. Maybe we can talk later."

"You bet, little guy. Have a good night's sleep and we'll go for a walk in the morning before we drive back to Seattle. Can you sleep okay with that collar?"

"Sure, I'm fine. G'night. See you in the morning."

Watching Angus over the next couple of weeks was fascinating. During the time he wore the collar, he did bump into things, but not because he couldn't see them. His depth perception was flawed because of the "lampshade" he wore, but once we were able to remove the collar, he moved like a sighted dog. The blind dog demolition derby that had raced through the yard was gone and in his place was a dog that walked around shrubs and plants instead of bulldozing right through them. When he was blind we called him "Bird Boy" because he loved chasing the birds, particularly the ravens and crows that teased him unmercifully. Now that he could see them, I often saw him staring at them without realizing what he was looking at until they made noise. Then he recognized what he was seeing and started to run after them. He was learning to use visual cues rather than just auditory signals.

It went like this for a while until one day at the beach the messages came together in a way that finally made sense to Angus. We were walking on the inside path at Henry's beach; by now he was able to be off leash like the other guys because the path was familiar and Joey and Fitz stayed with him. We were walking along and suddenly I saw Angus go into the marsh area that bordered the path. He'd never done this before, and I called him and asked him to come back. No response. I called again and started in after him. Soon I found that I couldn't see him; even worse, I couldn't get to him. He'd just disappeared. The water wasn't deep, but there were thick brambles and berry bushes that made it impossible for me to plow through. I kept looking for a way in and finally I found a break in the bushes and emerged on the other side in the marsh area. I kept calling to him as I lurched around in the marsh, but he didn't respond. I couldn't imagine where he'd gone in such a short time. I kept plodding on and finally I saw him in a little clearing. My immediate reaction was to slosh after him, but I saw that he was safe. What I heard and saw made me stop, listen, and watch.

I saw Angus, knee deep in water, standing in the middle of a flock of Canadian geese and a small group of ducks. Directly in front of them was a large blue heron that was stick-walking toward them. Not threatening, just walking slowly.

Angus didn't seem to be in any danger so I didn't move. Here was this small black dog surrounded by birds with an even bigger bird coming toward him. Angus stood with his back to me and I couldn't see his eyes, but I was sure they were wide open. But the question was: Did he know what he was seeing? I soon found out.

"Hey dog, what're you doing here? My lady and I have a nest here. This isn't your place." This from the heron who was still walking toward Angus.

"Sorry, guess I got lost. Didn't mean to get in your space. How do I get out of here?"

"Well dummy, how'd you get in?" One of the mallards swam toward him.

"I dunno. I was following my nose and I ended up here."

"Didn't you watch where you were going? This marsh is pretty deep in places. It's for us birds and not for dogs. You can't wander around out here without looking where you're going." One of the geese impatiently moved in toward Angus.

"Okay, okay, I wasn't looking I guess. Or, maybe I was looking but I didn't know what I was seeing. I dunno. Being able to see is new to me, and I still don't always know what I'm looking at. Gimme a break."

By now the heron was right in front of Angus, and he bent his long neck down to get a closer look at him. "Oh, I get it. You've got new eyes and you don't know how to use them. Is that it?"

"I guess. I'm used to finding my way by smell and sound."

One particularly large goose moved in closer and cocked his head toward Angus. "Maybe you're being lazy. Maybe you aren't exercising those eye muscles enough. I got hurt in one of my eyes last year and for a long time I didn't want to use it because it was easier to let the other one do the work. Maybe it's like that for you only it's easier to fall back on your ears and nose. I gotta tell ya though, if you've got eyes, you'd better use 'em.

Your nose and ears aren't always gonna get you out of places you don't know about. You have to look around."

Angus was listening intently, and he didn't move. At first I thought he wasn't going to respond, but then he turned away from the goose that'd spoken to him and waded a few steps closer to the heron and looked up at him.

"Wow, you're really big. Can you see better from up there?"

"No, I can see like you can. It's all the same. Just a different look that's all. Never mind me. Did you understand what the goose said to you? This is important."

"Yeah, I guess. I mean, I think you're maybe right. Since I got my new eyes I've been able to see, but I haven't been paying much attention. I have people and other dogs who look out for me, and I guess I figured I didn't have to do too much by myself. It's nice not bumping into stuff, but I haven't really been looking."

"Turn around, dog. Tell me what you see." The heron straightened his neck and waited while Angus turned around and looked in my direction.

"I see my friend, Dale. She's standing over there watching us."

I waved at Angus, but I didn't move or talk. In a moment of rare human insight, I sensed that I wasn't the teacher here.

"That's right. Now, I want you to tell her to go away. Tell her to go back to the path. Let her know that you'll join her there." The heron firmly directed Angus.

"But, I don't know how to get back there. I'm lost."

"No, you're not lost and you do know how to get back there. You have to use your eyes. Go on, tell her."

"Dale?"

"Yes, Angus, I hear you." I wanted so much to go to him, but I didn't move.

"Dale, you go back to the path. I'll … I'll find you."

"Okay, my friend, we'll be waiting for you." I quickly turned away before I could change my mind and made my way out of the marsh, through the brush and back to the path. Ellaine, Pip, Fitz and Joey were all milling around waiting for me. I told them that I'd explain in a minute and that Angus would be along shortly.

"But, where is he? Why didn't you bring him out with you? Is he okay?" Elaine was worried and couldn't understand why Angus wasn't with me. I couldn't understand why Angus wasn't with me either, but I somehow knew that he had to do this on his own, so I explained what I'd seen and heard.

We waited. It probably wasn't a long wait, but it seemed long. Joey, Pip and Fitz were calm, but Ellaine and I were pacing. We weren't in charge of this experience, and it was difficult to stand back and let Angus learn what he needed to know without our intervention.

Finally we heard a rustling in the bushes and Angus emerged. When he saw us, he came running over and raced around in circles.

"I did it! I did it! I looked where I was going and I found my way back. It was so neat. I didn't think I could, but those birds kept telling me I could and so here I am. I watched where I was going and I found you guys. I really was seeing. It's so great. I could smell and hear, but I had to watch where I was going and I did it. Let's keep going and see what else is here."

We gave Angus big hugs and continued our walk, watching our newly inspired dog look at his surroundings for the first time. I could almost see those messages flying back and forth from eyes to brain as he ran along the path. He'd go racing along and all of a sudden he'd see something that he wanted to investigate and he'd screech to a halt, go over and look, then sniff, and off he'd go again. While we were walking, the heron flew out of the marsh and landed on a piece of driftwood quite a ways down the path. Angus didn't hear him, but he certainly did see him. Even though the heron was quite a distance away from him, Angus raced over and stopped in front of him, tail wagging like crazy. He stayed for a minute and then came running back to us.

"That's my friend. Isn't he neat? He helped me. Can he come home with us?"

I laughed and picked him up and kissed him. "No, dear boy. He's at home here. He and his mate have a nest to protect. Besides, he wouldn't like living in a house. But, we can visit him when we come and walk here. Is that okay?"

"Sure, okay, if you think so." Then he was off again. He moved confidently and he didn't miss a thing. He really could see, and he knew what he was seeing.

It's been over three months now since Angus came home to live with us. His friends at Happy Hills have kept in contact with us, mostly through wonderful e-mail messages from Kitty, their webmaster. Cheryl and her staff loved him and are so happy he has a home and a family who love him too. Kitty even wrote a touching story, *"The Miracle of Angus,"* which was posted on their website. Angus says that he was okay being blind, and I believe that, but he shows us in every way that he feels more complete now that he can see. He says that his world fills him up and he's content. He's also become our new resident caregiver.

Not long ago it became clear to us that we needed to let Fitz continue his journey. We'd been watching him carefully, knowing that his thirteen year old body was shutting down on him. We didn't want him to stay around for us, which he would have done because he knew we needed him, but we couldn't allow him to sacrifice the quality of his life for us. After a day when he was unable to eat, we decided that it was time to help him on his way. That night, his last with us, Angus lay down next to him on the bed, getting as close as he could, and he wrapped both front legs around Fitz's neck and slept with him that way until morning. I'd wake up often during the night to be sure that Fitz was resting easy, and I'd see Angus snugged close to him, nose to nose, offering comfort and love. I knew that the position Angus was in wasn't comfortable for him, but I also knew that he was doing what he wanted to do. Fitz had been his anchor when he first arrived and he was returning the favor.

As I look at Angus, sleeping beside me as I write these words, I'm very clear about the fact that even though we made it possible for him to see, his ability to look at the world is his own gift to himself and to us. It may be true that the eyes are the windows of the soul, but without the desire to look through those windows, seeing isn't always believing.

Angus is a believer.

Chewy's Post

I thought he was lost. There wasn't a person in sight, and yet here was this cute fuzzy duck of a dog - black, kinda curly - just aimlessly (or so I thought) wandering around on the inside path at Henry's Beach. I suppose people who know breeds would say he was a Cockapoo. Or maybe a Schnauzapoo. Whatever.

"Hey guy! What're you doing? Are you here all alone?" I bent down to get a closer look.

There was a tentative wag of the tail and a blank stare. "C'mon lady. Look harder. I'm not alone; you're here. Your dogs are here. And, there's York, the heron. He's here. There's the ocean, rocks, driftwood, even the seagulls and sandpipers are here. Who's alone?"

"Well, I mean … don't you have a human companion here with you?"

"Sure, but she's way ahead with my brother. He's younger and can run faster, so I hang out around here and they pick me up on the way back."

By now, I was sitting on the ground, fairly close to him and I could see that he was an old guy. His eyes were clouded and his muzzle was gray. I was rubbing his ears as we talked. "Okay, but maybe I should wait here with you until she comes back. Just to be sure you're all right."

"Do I look like I'm not all right? I'm fine. We've been doing this beach walk for years, and even if I can't see very well with my eyes, I know exactly where I am. Please, don't worry. She'll be back. Go on with your walk." He gave me a quick slurp on my nose with his sandpapery tongue and turned away.

"I don't feel right just leaving you here. Why don't you walk with us and we can meet her?"

"Look, Dale. That's your name, right? I know you mean well, but I'm fine. Really, I am. I don't walk far any more, and it's better if I just sniff around here and check my mail. Go on. Please."

Finally acknowledging that he knew best, I gave him a hug, got up and continued down the path with Joey, Angus and Harper- my three Schnauzer friends.

It was one of those gorgeous fall days on the island; it was cool, but there was enough skinny sunshine to allow me to take off my heavy jacket. It was so clear that I could see the Canadian Rockies in the distance, and the harbor in Anacortes seemed only a few miles away. Mount Baker was "out," as they say here, and his top was gleaming like a marshmallow sundae. Well, not his whole top. After all, it was fall and the winter snows hadn't come yet, so only about half of the top was covered with snow. In another month or two, the marshmallow topping would be complete. For now, he looked lopsided.

I heard frogs in the marsh to my right and a flock of Canadian geese honked their way overhead. Another perfect formation. How do they do that? Usually they make a pit stop at the marsh but when I heard a gunshot, I understood why they were heading away from the marsh. Smart geese. It was hunting season again.

I stopped and quickly looked back toward my fuzzy friend to see if the sound of the gunshot had frightened him, but he never even raised his head so I guess he didn't hear the noise. He was probably hard of hearing too. I watched him for a bit, just to reassure myself that he was fine where he was, and after I saw him wandering around, sniffing, wagging his tail the whole time, I figured that he did know what he was doing.

Off in the distance I saw another person and a small dog coming toward us. The woman walked fast while her companion ran circles around her. The dog saw us first, and when he came closer I could see that he looked very much like my black fuzzy friend, only he was a lovely tan color. He ran up and enthusiastically greeted us.

"Hi! I haven't seen you guys here before. Did you pass my brother on the way?"

"Hi yourself, cute one. Yeah, we passed your brother a ways back."

By this time, the woman was close enough so that I could talk to her too without shouting. "Hi. Beautiful morning, isn't it?"

She smiled and stopped walking. "Sure is." A woman of few words.

"We met your other friend back on the trail. I thought he was lost at first, but he assured me that you'd be along soon and not to worry about him."

"Oh, that's Chewy. This is Chet, his adopted brother. Chewy doesn't walk fast any more; he goes as far as he can while Chet and I keep walking. We pick him up on our way back."

"That's what he told me. How old is he?"

"He's seventeen now. He can't see or hear well, but we've been coming here for years so he feels pretty secure. He loves this trail."

By now, since Chet was obviously anxious to move on, I smiled, told them it was nice to meet them and we continued on our way.

After that first meeting, we saw the woman (never did get her name), Chewy and Chet at the beach on a regular basis. We always smiled, said our hellos and then just went our separate ways. This went on for a couple of years until one day we saw the woman coming down the trail as we were returning and she was carrying Chewy. I watched her put him down and then continue toward us with Chet bouncing along ahead of her.

"I see that Chewy isn't walking well these days. Is he okay?"

"He's fine, but he can hardly walk anymore and I have to carry him. I don't want to leave him home though, because he knows when it's time for our walk and he loves it so much here. I figure he's safe until Chet and I come back. He sniffs around in his special place and when we catch up with him, I pick him up and carry him back to the car."

"Does he feel pretty well, other than not being able to move around much?"

"Oh, I take him to the vet whenever I think he might be uncomfortable, but the vet assures me that he isn't in any pain. He still loves to eat and he doesn't seem to be hurting, so I guess he's fine. He's just old and tired."

As we were talking, I watched Chewy and he was blissfully sniffing a particularly interesting piece of grass as he tottered around. He was unsteady on his legs, but he was where he wanted to be. For a fleeting second I wondered why she took Chewy to the vet to find out how he was rather than asking him, but I didn't follow through on that thought. None of my business.

I bent down and put my hand gently on Chewy's back so I didn't startle him. He didn't see anything any more. "Hey, buddy. How's it going? You okay?"

"Oh, hi Dale. I'm fine. Just a little unsteady, but I feel okay. I'll stay around as long as my friend needs me. Have a good walk. Don't worry about me." He gave me another one of his great dragonbreath kisses and turned away.

"Okay, my friend, enjoy yourself. See you later."

That day was the last time I saw Chewy until yesterday. For the next several weeks, each time we came to the beach, he wasn't there, nor was Chet or the woman. I kept wishing that I had gotten her name and phone number because I felt a strong urge to call and see if Chewy was still with us. But I hadn't and so I was unable to reach her to check on him. I suppose it says something about me that I could see someone on a regular basis for years and know the name of the dogs but not the person. So, we walked our walk, and every time I saw a black dog I hoped it might be Chewy, but it never was.

We saw all of the regulars though. Duffy the Scottie snuffled around, his short legs furiously digging as he rooted around under the driftwood looking for mice. Skookie, the American Eskimo, and Shad, the chocolate Poodle, were always there too. Skookie did warp factors on the path and sloshed around in the marsh while Shad poked along, never far from his human companion. One of my favorite visual treats was seeing Baby, a young Lab mix, playing with Moushi and Keico, two energetic Boston Terriers.

Baby was much larger than the pint-sized dynamic duo, but he always got down low enough on the ground to play without hurting them. Miss Coffee Bean, a gentle, shy Dalmatian with coffee bean colored spots moseyed along with her human friend, always trying to carefully avoid the rambunctious schnauzer boys that always wanted to play. She was too lady-like to indulge in such boisterous antics.

Ace, a smooth coated Collie, and Maggie, a Husky mix, walked sedately with their companion while Beau, a beefy black Lab, explored the driftwood and played with any dog that greeted him. I noticed that Franklin, the Border Collie, was walking slower and slower each day too. I knew he was about seventeen and wouldn't be making the walk much longer either. As much as I enjoyed seeing the regulars, I missed Chewy.

Finally, one morning many weeks after my last meeting with Chewy, we came to the spot on the trail that was his favorite place. There was a post dug into the ground with a letter-sized paper stapled to a piece of cardboard that was tacked on to the post. As we walked closer, I could see that on the paper was a picture of Chewy. Below the photograph were the words,

"IN MEMORY OF OUR BELOVED CHEWY WHO LOVED TO WALK AND SNIFF THIS TRAIL."

A scarf and a bunch of flowers lay beneath the post.

I felt such a mixture of emotions. I felt sad that Chewy wouldn't walk this beach (at least in physical form) again. I felt happy that he didn't have to deal with his tired old body any more. I felt guilty that I hadn't said goodbye to him the last time we had met. I felt compassion and sympathy for his woman friend because I knew that she must miss him terribly. And I felt such happiness to know that she had loved him so much that she had put up a memorial for him. Now, that's really being connected to your animal companion. She wanted everyone who walked this path to know about her friend and to remember him as she did.

I stood there for a long time looking at the photograph of Chewy. His friend must have taken the picture as he was sniffing the ground in this same spot. The picture had been taken when he was older too. I could see his gray muzzle and clouded eyes. He was smiling in the photograph. What a guy.

It's been months now since Chewy's memorial post was placed on the trail and a most wonderful kind of thing has happened. Every few days I see that something has been added to the memorial site. First there was another bunch of flowers. Then a few days later, I saw that someone had actually planted an Azalea at the base of the post. Some weeks ago a collection of seashells was arranged beside the scarf. Beautiful rocks were then placed near the shells. Last week a small wooden cross had been nailed to the top of the post. Yesterday there was a lovely piece of driftwood carefully nestled among the small rocks.

I've never actually seen anyone put objects near the post, but obviously people who walk the trail are touched by the memorial and feel compelled to add their remembrance to the spot. Maybe people who never even knew Chewy feel connected to him and want to offer a gesture of their sympathy and remembrance. I'm sure that the scarf and first bouquet of flowers were left by the woman, but she and Chet have never been back to the beach. I have a feeling that they've moved out of area. All of the other objects have been left by beach walkers. People leave their thoughts and feelings for a dog that has touched their hearts.

That's how it is here. I've seen people connect in what I call progressive beach art. One day somebody comes along and starts to build something out of the driftwood on the beach. Then the next day, or maybe even several days later, someone else adds his or her artistry to the initial effort. And so it goes. People want to connect. People need to create something together.

Nobody ever tears down someone else's creation. They add their imagination and a new facet appears. Someone even carved wooden birds, red, blue and brown, and tacked them on various pieces of driftwood. Neat. That's the way it is here.

Yesterday I saw Chewy again. No, not his physical form. But he was there. I felt and saw him as surely as if he'd been physically standing in front of me. We were approaching his post and I clearly saw him sniffing around the base. He looked terrific! He moved with an agility I'd never seen before, and he was wagging his tail in a kind of slow, easy motion. His eyes were clear and his muzzle was shiny black. This was a happy dog. I stopped and bent down to get his attention.

"Hey, guy, I've missed you. It's wonderful to see you looking so … healthy."

"Oh, hi Dale, it's good to see you too. What do you mean you've missed me? I know that you think of me every time you take this walk. How can you miss me if you think about me?"

"Good point. What do you think about all of these goodies that people have left here?"

"Great. I like it that people feel like they can join in. But, I wish they all didn't feel so sad. My energy still comes here a lot, and sometimes I feel people crying. I've seen you cry too. Why so sad?"

"Well, I guess my tears are there because I miss you. I know, you just said that because I think of you I don't really miss you, but maybe I'm missing the physical you. I'm learning to live without Ellaine's physical presence, and it's the hardest lesson I've experienced in this life."

"Trust me, Dale, you wouldn't want the physical me back again. Neither do I. Neither does Ellaine. My body was tired and worn out. I was eighteen years old! It was time to move on. This is much better. I get to continue my journey, like Ellaine is continuing hers. My energy comes back here whenever I want to visit, and I know that hers does too- here and at your house. It's very cool not having a body."

As I was thinking about him and smiling about the "very cool" phrase, I could see his image starting to fade. Within a matter of seconds, I couldn't see him any more. But I knew that my not being able to see him right then had nothing to do with him. It had to do with me. I believed him when he said that his energy came back quite often, and the fact that I'd never seen him before now had more to do with my limitations than his visibility. I think his image faded because somehow I understood that I didn't need to see him in the usual sense to know he was there.

That was yesterday. Today we walked the trail again, but it felt different to me. What felt different? Well, the best way I can explain would be to say that I felt lighter, and my feet didn't seem to drag as we approached Chewy's post. You see, up until today, even though I was always curious to see if there would be something new added to the memorial, I also felt reluctant to reach that spot because I knew I would feel sad. Today I didn't feel sad because I knew that it was as it should be that Chewy had moved on to his next expression of spirit. Today, for the first time, I wanted to add something to Chewy's post. I've been wondering what to add, but I couldn't come up with anything that felt right. Until now.

Tomorrow we'll go to the beach as we always do. And when we get to Chewy's post, I'm going to sit down and read this story to him. If I can see him, that will be wonderful. If not, that's okay too because I know he'll be there. My gift will be letting him know that I learned some very important lessons from him. Writing all of this down is my way of thanking him.

Learn everything you can.

Teach what you know.

We're all one.

Thanks, Chewy.

In Memoriam

With love and thanks for the *first light* experiences

Alba

Babette

Baron

Blue

Blue

Boo Boo

Casper

Chewy

Chouy

Cody

Cooper

Duncan

Easy

Fitz

Gus

Higgins

Jake

Jenny

Junior

Malinche

McKenna

Nakita

Pearl

Pip

Princess

Rosy

Satch

Shad

Sheba

Siam

Skookie

Socks

Sonny

Sushi

Swede

Tank

Thomas

Xander

Zippy

Joey

About the Author

Ardeth De Vries is a teacher, writer, and animal welfare advocate whose work with animals includes: three years of volunteering at an animal shelter, thirty years of rescuing abused and neglected Schnauzers, the operation of "Broken Arrow", a non-profit organization created to assist people with veterinary expenses for their companion animals, serving as end-of-life consultant, animal loss counselor and board member of Old Dog Haven, a non-profit organization that offers hospice care, assisted living and placement assistance for senior dogs, grief counseling for humans who are mourning the death of an animal friend, locating homes for animals in need, and teaching seminars and classes relating to animal welfare.

She lives with her Schnauzer family, Angus, Harper and Teddy, on an island in the Pacific Northwest, and has just completed an allegorical novel, *A Space Between*, about that "space between" lives. Currently she is working on a non-fiction book, *A Field Guide for Incoming Spirits*, which explores the difficulties involved in being human.